# THE SHADOW OVER PSYCHE STATION

YUVAL KORDOV

Ebook ISBN 978-1-997779-01-8

Paperback ISBN 978-1-997779-02-5



Cover by Victor Platon Jr.

I have seen beyond the bounds of infinity and drawn down daemons from the stars. I have harnessed the shadows that stride from world to world to sow death and madness.

H. P. LOVECRAFT, *FROM BEYOND*

# 1
# THE VOID

Marcus stared into the void, and the void stared back.

The shuttle window was tiny, only enough hard glass for a nominal view, but even so the imperial assessor always expected... more. Brilliant nebulae, rivers of cosmic dust, constellations as dense as the glimmering spaceport beacons on windswept Mars. Anything. Instead, there were only dim pinpricks of light, scant suggestions of life. All false, assuredly. A vast and empty ocean, punctuated by a handful of ramshackle human outposts.

The last of them.

The void had been his life for the last six months, transiting from Mars to the asteroid belt, then from one mining station to the next. Eros, Themis, Hygiea, Ceres—his prior stop, on whose shuttle he was currently riding under autopilot. Assessing, as assessors do, on behalf of a distant empire.

Mars was dying, cut off from Earth after the War, a mewling babe desperate for sustenance. The asteroid belt was its only lifeline, and that line had frayed to a thread. Shipments had slowed, loads were light or tainted. Particularly those from 16

Psyche, his current and much maligned final destination. It was his job to find out why.

*16 Psyche.*

A swell of nausea rolled through his guts, gurgling past the armor plates of his exosuit. He fiddled with the keys on his wrist terminal for the thousandth time, trying to get his compression settings just right. He never could, and his cramped accommodations didn't help. The shuttle's passenger compartment had barely enough room to stand and turn about, never mind stretch, designed as it was for cargo first, humans second or not at all. Compressing him, transmuting all emotions to anxiety.

"It's not right over there," the Ceres administrator had warned the morning before Marcus disembarked. They were floating together in the airlock, the man's knuckles white as he gripped the bulkhead, a viscous line of sweat seeping from his brow. It was unclear if his concern was for the assessor or his shuttle, but he hadn't been eager to release either.

Marcus always compartmentalized his scrutiny while on tour, rarely discussing the shortfalls of other stations. There were perceptions to maintain, after all. Each station must think the others to be in order, and the threat of military intervention —mostly an empty one, given the state back home—reserved only for them. But the outburst piqued his interest, given the criticality of local trade. Mining stations were as dependent on each other as Mars was on all of them. There was only so much onboard recycling capability, and the primary asteroids, however resource-rich, made Mars seem like Eden by comparison. Transport shuttles met every month at relay points between stations, swapping pilots and pleasantries along with their essential cargo.

But not Psyche Station.

"We haven't seen them in years," the man had admitted, a faraway look in his eyes as he shielded the pressure door controls with his body. "Last we did, they weren't right. Looked funny, smelled funny."

Not much of an assessment, especially to a professional assessor. That's what logs and an abundance of travel time were for. And the deeper Marcus delved, the more he found. Vague and disturbing reports from all the other stations, not just Ceres, intensifying as the years counted down. Errant behavior, belligerence toward local trade, accusations of heresy even. By the end of it, the reports verged on hysterical, declaring the inhabitants of Psyche Station no longer human. The last sighting described their shuttle pilot as gray-skinned, bloated in the middle, and gangly all around, like some sort of spaceborne octopod.

Just stories, surely.

Everyone out here suffered from an excess of darkness and a deficit of gravity. The void was a curse, erosive to body and mind. There was a regimen for it: drugs and exercise. And the near-Mars gravity of rotating station habitats helped when not traveling between them for weeks on end. But spinning around in space brought its own issues. They were all changed by it, even Marcus, especially him, allergic as he was to the standard pharmaceutical cocktail.

He had only his shiny white military-grade exosuit to compensate. It was an old Earth model, far superior to anything currently manufactured. Even so, climate control, mag boots, and the sophisticated compression layer beneath its armor plating could only do so much in microgravity. It had begun to feel too short, his custom-refit helmet too tight. Wherever mirrors presented themselves, he averted his gaze just in case. Truly, he was poorly suited to this task, his mind as disturbed in sleep as his body was when awake, wracked with dreams of floating naked in the dark. And yet he had volunteered, driven by some deep-seated yearning he had yet to identify.

Just stories... except for the station-to-station cargo manifests, which complained of the same issues as Mars-receiving: a peculiar sheen to the ore, luminescent when it should have been inert; an equally peculiar smell, like rotting fruit; and always underweight. As well as autonomous systems behaving strangely, prone to wandering off course despite no sign of damage to their circuitry.

Some of the reports were obviously exaggerated, but others required delicate separation of fact from fiction—the story of his life. In any case, Ceres had all but cut themselves off from their neighbors. Local trade was reduced and accomplished through autopilot, just as he was traveling now, trusting his life to a decrepit navigational computer.

Marcus stared out the window again, seeking the relay station where his shuttle would meet up with Psyche Station's. At that point, one of their pilots would board and manually transport him the rest of the way, as had been mandated in the original summons. There was nothing out there. Not yet. He was still a day away, but each idle minute brought more trepidation.

*16 Psyche.*

Named after the Greek goddess of the soul. Thought by scientists to be the core of an ancient protoplanet, obliterated at the dawn of the solar system.

Cast out.

He was not the superstitious type, but it didn't take long in space to start seeing monsters in every shadow, clinging to every lumen of manmade light for succor. What sort of malignancy did the ancient rock carry, festering over billions of years? What curse had it laid on the souls of those who mined it?

Marcus brought up a pixelated image of the asteroid on his heads up display, thumbing the directional pad on his wrist terminal to rotate it this way and that. An ugly thing from any angle: ovoid, pockmarked, a blot of diffuse green streaked with throbbing veins of rust and dull gold.

He tapped through an adjacent menu, pivoting the perspective around to focus on Psyche Station. It was the first of the mining outposts, now almost forty years old. A cylindrical core attached by four thick spokes to a habitat ring, 170 meters in diameter according to the readout, docking ports on the "bottom" and insectoid antennae bristling from its head. The whole thing spun on its axis, locked in place over 16 Psyche as though by an invisible tether, the two conjoined in a slow dance around the sun.

There were only five of the original six stations left, transporting their precious goods via automated drone across long and ponderous space lanes. Should that number drop any further, the result would be disastrous. There were no new technological advances, no new colonies, no help from the homeworld, only ever-increasing demand. Mars, once pitched as a second Earth, was falling toward entropy.

He zoomed into the rotating avatar, squinting as though the station's malicious inhabitants might reveal themselves through the windows. Tabbing through each of its cargo drones, seeking trails of leaking gas or debris—telltale signs of malfunction. There would be none, of course, as this image was conjured from the original schematics, but the longer he looked the faster his pulse, as though something might yet break through the simulation.

"Enough, already," he muttered.

Soon he would be there and could download all the local logs he needed. Until then, the third party reports were just conjecture, which served no one. If anything, it was probably time to rotate out some of the other station staff.

He brought up a series of file windows on his HUD, shuffling through dozens of incomplete spreadsheets and evaluations until he found his most recent draft recommendations, then held down the dictation key on his wrist. "Review personnel tenures, cross-reference with anomalous reports, and suggest rotations."

A new text line appeared after an empty checkbox, below a stack of other unchecked to-dos. He should have been caught up by now, but time flowed differently in transit. He started each day reviewing logs, only to find himself staring out the window hours later with little work completed, followed by exhaustion and restless sleep. The dreams, maybe. Even as his total sleep time incremented up, his fatigue worsened.

Marcus flipped up his visor and doffed a gauntlet to rub at his eyes. The cabin air was thin and tainted by the malodor of alien minerals. He breathed through his mouth as wan knuckles pushed against his eyeballs and long fingers clawed at the stubble along his jaw. He needed a shower and a shave.

A jagged fingernail caught on his neck and drew blood. He withdrew the hand and stared at it, struck for a moment by its appearance: too long, smooth fingers removed of their color. Though affixed to his body, it seemed autonomous, treacherous, like one of the rogue mining drones. With some effort, he commanded it back into its glove and dropped his visor down, breathing deeply as climate control kicked in.

The draft file was still centered on his HUD. He scanned the prior entries, blinking away a brief bout of double vision. But even as his eyesight returned to normal, he realized the to-dos on the last page were all the same, nearly to the word. He had been repeating himself.

He closed the file with a hard tap on his terminal, swallowing back a rising lump in his throat. It was almost eighteen hundred hours anyway—bedtime. He spared a final glance out the window, blinking away afterimages of an ugly green ovoid pulsing in the pitch, then shut his eyes.

# 2
# RELAY

*THE ONCE-MAN FLOATS over the surface of the asteroid. Cheeks puffed out, lips pressed shut, spindly arms and legs blowing in the cosmic breeze. Naked, wrapped in the black velvet of the void.*

*He has no sense of propulsion, yet is clearly moving, weaving through canyons of viridian metal too far removed from the sun to shimmer. The alien ore pulses instead, throbbing like a bioluminescent lifeform shackled to the lowest abyss, sighing unintelligible whispers as he skims its peaks.*

*Luring him deeper.*

*Something waits beyond the horizon, sheltered beneath a great iron mountain. It calls to him, but the sound is muffled.*

*He delves deeper, into spider vein trenches, caressing ancient wounds that have never healed. Gliding along narrow streams of ochre that bubble from the surface like pus, and jagged clefts whose deepest shadows stir at his passing.*

*But no matter how far he travels, he cannot see it.*

*The surface changes. Canyons straighten into a maze of cuts whose walls glitter with impossible geometries. One line ends, forcing him back, only to be turned around again. The call fades as he spirals deeper into the labyrinth.*

*He flounders. Cold creeps in. Pain explodes from every capillary. Until the last breath is expelled from his lungs.*

*The once-man, now a man again, screams into the void.*

"Approaching relay. T-minus sixty seconds to full stop."

Marcus gasped awake. Warning lights blared across his HUD, along with an incessant beeping. He strained to focus, dredging his senses back from the dream. Blurred digits floated in space, each segment brighter than the distant sun—his heart rate. 160BPM.

Gloved hands fumbled at his visor, but he twisted away from them, pressing his armored back into the recliner.

162.

He shut his eyes again, beating back hazy afterimages of the asteroid. Focusing on the rush of air entering his nose and leaving his mouth. Imagining that the roar of the shuttle's decelerating engines was the sound of his lungs, sucking back oxygen as fast as his suit could cycle it.

The beeping slowed.

The orange glow pressing upon his eyelids dimmed.

He opened his eyes.

Something glinted outside the window, obscured by the jumble of medical warnings on his HUD. He smashed at his wrist terminal to dismiss them, but by the time they were gone, the shuttle had rotated around, reorienting itself for continuous thrust to Psyche Station. Fumbling apart his safety harness, he pressed away from his recliner to crane around the tiny viewport—too late.

Something was out there, but on the other side of the vessel. The relay, but what about his rendezvous?

"T-minus 30 seconds," the shuttle's unbothered female voice intoned.

His heart began to pound again as fear wormed into his chest, that all the reports of Psyche Station were true, understated even. Or that he would be left alone out here with a dullard computer, unable to carry him back to civilization if the codified steps weren't followed exactly.

He fell back into his seat and pulled his data jack from his wrist terminal, then tried and failed to plug it into the recliner port. His hand was shaking. Two tries and three curses later, he snapped it into place. A progress bar popped up on his HUD, filling at a ponderous rate as his suit interfaced with the shuttle's preoccupied systems.

A sickly wail echoed through the cabin, followed by a chorus of metallic pings and the pitter-patter of structural settling all down the hull. Marcus flinched, gripping the armrests tighter, willing every uninspected rivet to hold fast. The progress bar accelerated to a finish just as the shuttle went quiet, presumably now stationary alongside the relay.

"Docking in progress," the shuttle said.

With the relay or another shuttle?

A new chorus beat against the hull, sending the walls of his module chattering. Scrapes along the shuttle's too-thin skin and a sequence of hammer strikes.

The shuttle menu popped up in front of him.

Marcus stabbed at the Exterior Feed link, switched to full screen, then tapped through to the first camera: empty space.

Next: a quarter view of the relay, weak sunlight trickling along its parched solar panels.

The third camera panned over the relay's underbelly, where the shuttle's umbilical had just wriggled its way into a coupling.

He tapped to the last one and recoiled as an expanding transit chute filled his visor, slipping past the camera until there was only a narrow tunnel ahead. A final gong marked engagement with the shuttle's starboard passenger hatch.

Cold sweat soaked his palms, an emulsion of relief and nervous anticipation.

Dim yellow lights flickered along the steel crosshatch of the chute's frame. A red strobe followed, then a hard rush of air as the passage pressurized and snapped taut.

The opposing craft's outer door waited on the other side. It seemed miles away, dark save for a dull green glow along the door seams. His heart rate ticked up again. The sound of his own ragged breath drowned out everything else.

The door juddered open, slowly as though reluctant to dispatch its crew. A cloud of sparkling dust unfurled into the chute. Marcus wrinkled his nose as phantom smells clawed at his nostrils, conjured by Ceres' reports and the sudden recall of one of his first assessment jobs back home: a failed apple orchard, the last of its kind, sweltering under a sweet fog of rot. Giant bacteria inundating the soil as cosmic radiation seeped through the domes. His superiors had demanded guilty parties, but no one did anything wrong; it just wasn't meant to be.

A hand thrust out from the shadow to grip the edge of the doorframe. He toggled the zoom to get a better look, but the resolution was pitiful under low light. The rest of the body followed, barely backlit by a recessed strobe and stretched thin by the camera's wide-angle lens. Static crackled at the edges of his HUD, bleeding chromatic aberrations across the image. He strained to see a scalp writhing with tentacles, but the head that entered the chute was as smooth as the body.

The pilot was wearing a spacesuit, as required by protocol.

Marcus swallowed. Of course he was.

With a final push, the figure sailed head-first into the chute. Marcus held his breath, waiting to see the face. It drifted closer, helmet filling the frame. Then jerked up.

A gaunt face and black eyes behind a partially polarized visor.

Ugly, but human.

Then gone again.

Marcus fell back into his recliner. With a tap on his terminal, he brought up his suit's pharmaceutical inventory. Though he couldn't take anything to directly offset microgravity, there was no shortage of sedatives. As well as hypnotics, analgesics, stimulants, prokinetics, laxatives, and a host of other onboard "assistance" to cope with his long tour.

The shuttle let loose a groan as the passenger airlock cycled. He dismissed the inventory window, slowed his breath through force of will alone, and stared back at the now-retracting chute.

The body of the alien shuttle rolled inward from the edges of the screen as the passageway was reabsorbed into its hull. Dull metal skin patched over so many times that it confused the eye, flashing green between blinks. Tiny windows that matched his own, dark as the void. It would travel by autopilot all the way to Ceres, as he had here, to deliver its dubious cargo. Even so, he stared at the nearest window, zooming in again in case he might spot someone left behind—or something. There was only slithering distortion, black on black.

He closed the window, navigated to Interior Feed, then clacked away until he found a camera directed at the airlock. A line of ceiling lights flickered slowly awake to direct the pilot to the cockpit, producing more static than illumination. He drummed anxious fingers on his armrest, stopping when a shadow crept out from the edge of the screen: exploratory, one long tendril becoming five, stretching across the deck and up the opposing wall, then snapping back into a monolith as the pilot finally emerged.

Marcus zoomed in again, following the man's zero-g lurch from one handhold to the next, booted feet flapping behind his lanky body as though swimming through some hidden astral medium. Gliding past low bulkheads and netted cargo, until he was perched right outside the habitation module.

There was another camera there, above the door. If Marcus switched to it now, he would have a full view of the pilot.

Protocol demanded acknowledgment.

He paused, one hand hovering over his terminal as he turned to face the thin wall that separated them. A wedge of green caught his eye—the door was unlocked. Goosebumps prickled along his neck and scalp as he debated between a leap for the deadbolt and opening a channel.

The man hovered in place, waiting.

Marcus shut off the camera feed, stretched his jaw until his tongue stopped wagging uselessly in his mouth, then tapped open ship comms. "Marcus O., Imperial Assessor." His voice sounded like someone else's, rendered unfamiliar by disuse. "Requesting transit to Psyche Station for scheduled audit."

There was no reply save for a liquid burble and a chattering hiss that sounded like distant whispers. He considered the door-cam again, then flinched as the module wall flexed with the pull of the exterior handhold. The pilot was on his way, his passage marked by fading vibration.

Quickly canting sideways, Marcus turned the lock and sighed in relief at the sight of red. He wanted to follow up with a comforting pronouncement, like "very good," or "that's that," but rising superstition stayed his voice. He peered around his cabin. There was an old Earth custom of touching wood to dispel evil, but no such material existed here, or really anywhere, anymore. Maybe that's why Mars Colony had been so unlucky, built as it was out of alien ore. Instead, he leaned back and visualized a pre-flight checklist. Assuming protocol was maintained, he'd have an hour to launch.

Recalling the umbilical, he brought up his inbox in case there had been any messages waiting for him at the relay. There were. The unread mail counter ticked up: seventy-eight, seventy-nine. Downloading into his suit alongside his incomplete to-dos, and a series of draft reports that had shrunk in length—and quality, if he was to be honest—as his tour wore on. The counter stopped at ninety-three. He yanked out his data jack and watched it slowly spool back into his forearm.

It would be three days' travel to 16 Psyche, which suddenly felt unbearable. He wanted to be there, or better yet done his tour and headed back home. Not pretending to work in this steel coffin with the void pressing in. His superiors insisted he should have adapted by the second station at the latest, but his agoraphobia only worsened with each new transit, alternating between suffocation within his cabin and the open terror of the void. And yet it was out there that his dreams carried him, like some sort of celestial fetus waiting to be born.

He tapped open his medical readouts: all normal. Good thing the suit couldn't read his thoughts.

Marcus sighed and took in the full extent of his cabin, spartan by any measure.

To his left, beneath the tiny window, was a life support module with a waste tube and nutrient tube—best not to mix those up. The menu included various flavors of macro-balanced paste, none of which originated on Mars. Strawberry, vanilla—words out of a dead language. And Salisbury steak, but Marcus had no idea what a "Salisbury" was. The lack of response from his stomach suggested no rush to find out.

To the right, the door, which he checked again to ensure it was locked. It was, though the flimsy walls of his compartment could probably be beaten down with little effort. He tried not to think about that.

Behind him, a single hard-shell suitcase with suit supplies and toiletries. One could never be sure about the hygienic practices of mining stations. Some of the chemists on Themis had taken to producing their own soaps and lotions using local clays.

The place reeked of ammonia and synthetic floral compounds. He had kept his suit on the whole time.

Then there was his recliner, which doubled as workstation and bed, though sometimes it felt more like a gurney.

He tapped open the Media menu on his HUD. Vids weren't transmitted this far out due to bandwidth limits, and fiction held little interest for him, particularly the pastoral Earth romances that had saturated the market lately. Instead, he navigated down to News, glancing idly at the headlines from the relay dump. They were all bad.

He shut the interface.

This was why he worked while in transit: not just because it was his job, but because it was the only thing sufficiently consuming to block out the reality of his situation, and reality in general. But even that had been taken from him, figures and calculations floating unmoored in his head, carrying him *out there*.

He opened the interior camera feed again, switching locations until the cockpit appeared. The pilot was settling in, working to restore manual control and performing all the obligatory system checks any normal pilot would. Marcus stared at his back, waiting... for what? He watched for several more minutes, thought of opening a communication channel to confirm the proper protocols were being followed, reconsidered, then turned off the feed as bored agitation took over.

A yawn pulled at his jaw, even though he had just woken up. Not surprising. Travel through space was an abomination at the best of times. The absence of a circadian cycle wreaked havoc on the brain, and his dreams didn't help matters. There had been experiments back in the early, pioneering days of colonization, but cryo sleep and the like remained the stuff of science fiction.

Luckily, he had his suit.

Marcus tapped open his pharmaceutical inventory again, navigating down to Hypnotics. They guaranteed a dreamless sleep at the cost of a wicked hangover, but there were drugs for that too. Duration could be set by stacking doses, though he had never exceeded a single "night" before. He toggled over to the plus icon and slowly tapped three times. It shifted from green to yellow to a warning amber, but the onboard computer didn't stop him. Three days of peace at the press of a button. He just had to sort out his other bodily functions first.

He glanced over at the life support module, trying to remember the last time he ate. His appetite had all but evaporated since starting this last leg of his tour, and confinement to a recliner didn't help. His suit would apply a hydration drip in any case, along with a steady stream of forced air and whatever else his comatose body needed. That said, he did want to relieve himself before going under. Mark I exosuits were entirely capable of processing waste via an integrated girdle, but shitting his pants didn't ever feel right, or good.

Returning to the main pharmaceutical menu, he popped a fast-acting laxative, flinching as a contact patch pricked along his abdomen. He would have thirty minutes, tops, but based on the gurgling of his already anxious bowels, probably less.

With a triple check of the door lock, he clambered from his recliner and set to detaching his posterior armor plates and compression flap. It was laborious, especially in such tight quarters: fumbling about blindly, bouncing off bulkheads, then biting down a yelp as his privates were exposed to the shuttle's icy climate. With little time to spare, he grabbed the waste tube and proceeded to empty himself fully and noisily into its funnel. A tiny bidet popped out to ensure he was sanitary, but it did nothing to allay his embarrassment. He wondered if the sound had carried all the way to the cockpit. As though in response, the shuttle's engines sprang to life at just that moment. He replaced the tube and hurriedly sealed himself back up.

"Ten minutes to launch," the shuttle announced. "Please ensure all safety harnesses are latched and cargo stowed."

A countdown appeared on his HUD uninvited. There would be no crush, no melting into his recliner like with a ground launch—he hated those. Just a steady and constant acceleration until the braking phase, at which point the shuttle would turn about. Even so, it made him queasy, empty guts or not.

Marcus eased the recliner back, but not so low that he lost sight of the window. A handful of stars glimmered in the distance, beckoning to him from the edge of Creation. Time wavered. The engines keened. The whole hull trembled, every panel and bone in his body vibrating, until it felt like he might dissolve, a star on the verge of collapse.

With a final glance at the door, he triggered the hypnotics.

# 3

# APPROACHING PSYCHE STATION

A SOUND.

Muffled trumpeting on the other side of a barrier. Seven long notes, stretched through time, like heralds of the end of days: fire falling from the sky; mountains turned to plains and seas boiled into deserts.

No, those things had already come, and humanity persisted. Only the demons were left, clawing from bottomless viridian pits—

It squawked again, dissonant. Someone talking.

He was awake.

He? Floating in the starless void.

Awake, but shut out. Flailing, until something sparked within the black: an injection, forcing awareness into his cells. Stuck synapses spooled back up, dredged from the deep. Sputtering fireworks bloomed into a latticework of light and thought.

He: Marcus.

Basic sensations returned, then—slowly, painfully. His hearing first, through wobbling eardrums.

Yes, the sounds were syllables, words, but he still couldn't make them out. There was too much distance between them, too much interference from the gale of forced air blowing against his nostrils, keeping his airway open. Too much weight everywhere, rolling along his body like storm-tossed waves as his suit coaxed him back into the world of the living. But also on his face, pressing his eyeballs back into his laggard brain.

Marcus tried to open his eyes, but they were fused shut. One budged halfway and filled immediately with burning tears. If he strained too hard, his corneas would shear off against eyelids turned to sandpaper.

His mouth, then. Stuck as well, but not as bad. His lips resisted at first but eventually gave way at the cost of several lashings of skin. Metal filled his mouth, a sharp tang on his teeth, gums, tongue, the back of his throat. Aftertaste from the hypnotics or dried blood—probably both. He couldn't swallow yet, but the airflow eased as his suit's life support systems sensed a new orifice.

He tried his eyes again. The left one craned open, still watering, the right one less eager to join but eventually breaking through three days' worth of rheum. Blurred shapes joined the blurred words, floating directly above him.

He blinked repeatedly, trying to clear his vision. His body still hadn't come fully online, just prickles so far, but at least he could almost see, almost hear. There was little smell on account of desiccated nasal passages.

The heavenly bodies slowly took shape: two arms, floating above him like wraiths, long fingers curled. He could feel the stretch through his armpits now, the slosh of stale blood pulsing back and forth. He willed them down, but the signal was weak, lingering at elbows grown stiff from disuse. Finally, they complied, folding into repose against his armor.

Fine motor control came next. A hand, then a finger. Enough for a clumsy sequence on his wrist terminal. A hydration tube whined up from beneath his chin and into his chapped lips. He took an awkward sip, then choked as weightless globules bounded along the back of his throat. Too tired to curse, he shut his eyes in concentration, tried again, and managed a few drops. The electrolyte-infused slurry was tasteless, but it woke his slumbering salivary glands, cooling the sting in his cheeks as he kept sipping. After a minute, he pried open his eyes.

Something was still floating around. Out there. Beyond the window.

Marcus tapped off his HUD, relocated his spinal vertebra, then tried to inch up, but his body wasn't ready yet. Heat flashed from throat to scalp. Panicked arms gripped the armrests of his recliner—vomiting into his helmet would be even worse than soiling his pants. Just as he thought of trying for his terminal, another injection pricked his abdomen. His suit was taking charge, dispensing antiemetics. He breathed through the war now waging in his guts, recruiting every ounce of willpower to seal off his throat until the sensation passed.

His helmet chimed with incoming comms.

"Approaching Psyche Station," the shuttle announced.

They were here.

He had to see, whether his body was ready or not.

He tapped his terminal back open and dispensed a cocktail of analgesic and stimulant. The jabs barely registered as a wave of energized euphoria spread through his veins, granting temporary reprieve from his malaise. A crash would come later, but he could re-up after getting settled, or maybe even recover in a proper bed.

Gritting his teeth, he toggled his recliner to an upright position. It still hurt, but the pain languished in the background now, and his stomach remained quiet. Once again, the window was empty. They must have been approaching from above the station, which in turn hovered above 16 Psyche like a terrestrial mosquito draining its host. He raced through his suit menus and brought up a ventral camera view, anxious blood pounding in his ears.

There it was: Psyche Station.

A great steel cruciform hanging in the void, bristling with antennae at its head, and haloed by a stained and scoured habitat ring. Some patches of the hull were so blackened that the whole thing seemed to slip in and out of the void. Spinning counterclockwise as though churning backward in time.

*Counterclockwise.*

Marcus blinked to make sure his eyes weren't playing tricks on him. It had spun clockwise in the diagram; he was sure of it. Something to double-check later.

There were no other co-orbital craft, no signs of life beyond the slow pulse of navigation beacons amidst its antennae. The windows were as dark as in the simulation. Altogether, it looked more like a relic than an outpost.

The shuttle banked down, making for the dock on the underside of the station's central hub. He held his breath as 16 Psyche crept into full view, shaped steel giving way to raw iron. It had been there the whole time, of course, but his brain hadn't been ready, blotting out the ancient planetoid until there was no choice. It looked just as it had in his dreams, only darker, dull green against the black like an infrared imaging anomaly on his visor. Scant sunlight battled with shadow over its uneven surface. Veins of muted color flashed in and out of existence then fell away into one great swirling abyss after another.

Vertigo lapped at his guts. He gripped the recliner with one hand, zoomed with the other, searching for some sign of the mining operation on the opposite pole. A handful of tiny silver dots buzzed about the edge of the feed, along with a growing chromatic aberration that might have been a debris cloud. He tried to zoom in more, but the camera was already maxed.

His helmet chimed again. "Commencing docking maneuvers."

The shuttle groaned as its reaction control thrusters ignited, turning the craft about while also matching Psyche Station's rotation. It would dock via the primary nose coupling beneath the cockpit.

Marcus tapped off the feed and leaned back in his recliner, glad for his empty stomach. The last time he had watched a docking procedure—in that case, Hygiea Station's spin steadily slowing, then replaced by a spinning star field—it left him dizzy for hours. Reacclimating to centripetal gravity would be bad enough.

He considered thumbing on a view of his enigmatic pilot, to ensure a by-the-book operation, but the growing rattle of the habitation module kept his arms fixed. He tried to close his eyes, but the fully metabolized stimulants in his bloodstream pried them back open. So, he passed the time scanning his document folders, applying superficial scrutiny to already completed assessments while glossing over the unfinished ones, careful not to get distracted by the shifting pinpricks of light outside.

The minutes dragged, stretched by his deliberate focus on the glowing text of his HUD, until an echoing boom snapped him back to the present. A metallic wail followed as the shuttle's hull torqued a fraction more to match its berth.

They had arrived.

He couldn't resist a quick glance out the window, but he tried to focus on the station's mottled bulkheads instead of the turning void.

The overhead lights guttered, snapped off, then returned slightly dimmer as power transfer completed. The steady, high-pitched hum he had long since stopped hearing wound down into a slow, resonant bass. Everything was still—almost. A rhythmic vibration pressed against the soles of his deactivated mag boots. If he ignored it, he could pretend he was back on Mars, safe and relatively secure belowground. But he wasn't. Not even close.

His helmet comms came alive again, but absent the cheery chime. Instead, static burbled on the line.

Marcus waited, every hair on the back of his neck standing at attention.

"Proceed to Admin," a voice intoned, the words thick and strangely enunciated, as though the speaker was just now breaking a years-long vow of silence.

He didn't have to be told twice. Marcus unclasped his harnesses in short order and pushed off, floating toward the ceiling. Simulated gravity wouldn't kick in until he moved out from the hub into the habitat ring, but given the miserable state of his body, it seemed wise to start walking now. He gripped a handhold on the cabin wall and forced his legs back to the floor, then tapped on his boots. They locked into place, followed by the whine of servomotors and the popping of joints as his suit micro-adjusted its posture. He was grateful for that.

He slow-stepped around the recliner to retrieve his suitcase. Dislodged from its netting, it banged noisily about the cabin, drifting in every direction except "down." The tiny abode that had been his home since leaving Ceres Station seemed impossibly small now, when standing. Only the locked door loomed large.

Marcus chewed the inside of his cheek, propped the case between his legs, then ran a suit diagnostic sequence from his wrist terminal—just in case it was open void out there. A progress bar popped onto his HUD, accompanied by reams of scrolling text. He allowed himself some basic stretches while it completed: neck circles, shoulder rolls, anything he could do to restore mobility while keeping an eye on the door.

The diagnostic completed with all systems green.

Fixing his jaw, he grabbed up his gear, unlocked the door, paused, then slid it open.

Nothing leapt out at him.

He wasn't sucked into space.

There was only the empty corridor, lit by the same ceiling lamps that had directed the pilot to the cockpit and the docking interface below. He stepped out, boots clanging on the deck as he followed the light. Small tufts of fog bloomed and faded near the bottom of his visor as he found his breath.

Walking felt alien. His calves burned even though his suit was doing the brunt of the work, and his feet were mostly numb. Luckily, or not, the way wasn't long. There were only two other compartments to navigate, each enclosed behind a broad bulkhead door. He took his time, hesitating before each button press to open the way, and flinching whenever a door sliced shut behind him.

The final door was inset with thick windows, offering a glimpse of the docking compartment beyond. He inched forward, pressing his visor against the glass. He knew what to expect; this shuttle was similar enough to all the other shuttles he had ridden in, as was the station beyond. Even so... readiness was a virtue.

He let go his suitcase and raised his arms to either side of his helmet to block out the glare. The room looked empty, its near side dark, the far end pulsing amber beneath hazard lamps ensconced in the wall. Adjacent the inner door, somewhere within the shadows, would be the access ladder to the cockpit.

He lowered his arms and tapped on local comms. A chattering hiss burbled in his ears. He tried to clear his throat, but it was still too dry.

"Confirm departure in two days," he croaked.

That was the plan. Verification was also a virtue.

There was no pickup on the other side. Instead, a general

acknowledgment ping flashed onto his HUD. Irregular, but it would have to do. Even so, he waited, peering up into the darkness to see if the pilot also planned on disembarking, or if he was going to stay here for the duration. His burning eyes eventually gave out.

"Okay then," he muttered.

Backing up a step, Marcus pressed the button adjacent the door. It juddered in place for a moment, then split down a hexagonal seam and rumbled into the wall. The warning lamps glared, triggering his visor to partially polarize. A mist of stray decontamination fluid billowed outward, licking at his boots and up his legs; the floor was thick with it.

Snatching up his suitcase, he marched forward but steered clear of the access ladder. His heart thudded with each magnetized step, eyes drawn to the ceiling hatch—still closed.

A tendril of fog slid across his darkened visor. He paused to wave it away, but the movement only summoned more. Somewhere in the back of his mind he noted a likely violation of HVAC maintenance schedules, but the rest of him bristled with anxiety. His skin felt clammy, as though the humidity was passing right through his armor.

He lurched forward and promptly slipped, pirouetting on one foot to slam into the wall.

A face stared back.

Marcus yelped.

Warning tones blipped in his helmet as flailing arms surrounded him. He scrambled backward, trying to push off, but they wrapped around him more tightly, hauling him in. He pushed even harder, until the assistive joints in his combat suit kicked in, translating panic to violence. With a whir and a snap, he was wrenched free.

He staggered backward, an alcove looming ahead.

Bulging, deep-set eyes stared from the darkness: his own eyes, magnified in the curved visor of a tethered spacesuit.

Marcus doubled over, huffing and blinking to exorcise the black spots from his vision. Airflow ticked up within his helmet as his suit tried to help. He was lucky to have it, probably still alive because of its constant attention, but in this moment shame outweighed gratitude. He wondered if the shuttle pilot had watched the whole thing, chortling to himself on the other side of the bulkheads.

He pushed himself back to standing and tapped on his helmet light. The fog recoiled, slithering down and away into the main body of the shuttle. After staring at his reflection a moment longer, he turned about. His suitcase was gyrating against the outer hatch, eager to leave. He couldn't blame it.

Squaring his shoulders as best as he was able, Marcus made his way toward the exit and into Psyche Station.

## 4

# CENTRAL RECEIVING

DECONTAMINATION TOOK FOREVER. Like most deep space operations, it had to be extremely thorough. And automated. Not because the empire espoused a deep trust of computers—that was a malady particular to private industry—but because of manpower, or lack of it. There were too many protocols to follow, with too many consequences in the event of a mistake. Reliance was inevitable, but prohibitions against artificial intelligence ensured that such systems were simple and predictable, even if that meant a skipped process could leave humans hanging.

Or trapped.

The second time the spray-and-vac process ran, Marcus started to worry. The third time, he was sure he'd live out the rest of his short life there. It was like the relay all over again. Luckily, there was no fourth cycle. Instead, the interior door shook open, the last bits of sterile foam dispersing into the vast chamber of the central hub.

Suddenly freed, he took a moment to compose himself. First impressions were everything, recognition of his authority imperative. All the admins he had encountered so far were cordial—

afflicted by their isolation, mentally or physically, but cooperative. Their livelihoods were on the line after all. Given the legends surrounding Psyche Station, he wasn't sure what to expect, only who: Administrator Octavia Marshall, female, sixty-five years old.

Her profile hovered near the bottom of his visor. She had been here since day one, part of the original crew that transported the station from the Moon, and from what he could tell from his briefing notes, had never left.

Until now.

The receiving area was empty. No administrator. No aide in her place. No message waiting on the control pad, not even a hand-scrawled note. Irritated, Marcus marched out of the bay—into chaos.

The central hub was huge, twenty meters across and four times as long, yet there was barely room to move. Its crisscrossing structural beams were swallowed by a spiraling maze of cargo netting and modular walls. Spotlit workstations protruded at random angles from every plane, stalactites and stalagmites both. Skeletal drone parts shimmied in their bindings, some dead, others aglow, hopefully with electricity and not radiation.

Worse, as he tried to follow the airlock transfer rail into the labyrinth, he realized he was walking "upward" and that 16 Psyche lurked behind him. The asteroid exerted almost no gravity, especially at this distance, but he could feel it tugging at his soul. A kernel of dizziness bloomed in his inner ear. Already, his body wanted to twist away from his legs, and it would only get worse once he was in the habitat ring.

He grabbed at the nearest control pedestal to steady himself, scanning the area for something to fix his attention on. There wasn't enough horizon to work with, but the guide rails ahead were mostly unobstructed. Keeping his eyes low, he trudged forward, focusing on the marionette-like motion of his legs as they lifted, lowered, adhered, lifted, lowered, adhered. Then to his boots, tracing the battle scars along the toe boxes and soles.

How many times had they carried someone into hostile territory? Or run from it?

Each armored footfall was accompanied by an echoing, solitary clang.

He paused a moment, holding his breath and listening intently as the chorus of steps receded. No whine of power tools or hammering of machinery accompanied them. The chamber, however chaotic in appearance, was silent.

He hadn't noticed at first, accustomed to his helmet's noise attenuation. Opening his terminal, he toggled the setting down. The station's pulse immediately beat against his ears: arrhythmic, punctuated with rattles and groans. But there were no sounds of human activity.

Scrutinizing his surroundings more carefully this time, he found the bays empty, the instruments sitting idle.

On lunch?

A glance at his HUD chronometer showed 11:27 MTC, too early for the standard break allotted to belt mining crews.

The first infraction, then.

Thinking about the rules steadied him. Protocols were a torch in the dark. Reinvigorated, he picked up the pace. Even as detours forced him up and down adjacent walls, he found his way back onto the path. He just had to keep moving.

Eventually, the cargo line would deposit him at Central Receiving, then the transit spokes into the habitat ring. The gateway between hub and ring was always manned, though he expected the attendant to be out of breath after a rushed return from the mess hall. A bevy of suitable admonishments swirled through his head.

Rounding the last obstacle—a corral of sheet metal seemingly purpose-built to obstruct traffic—he came upon the workstation in question.

Empty.

His throat tightened. "Where is everyone?" he growled—to himself, apparently.

A semicircular desk loomed up front, a wall of server racks behind it, their status LEDs blinking out meaningless patterns. Lifeless monitors slouched at either side of a peeling leatherette chair. The steel desktop was bare. No keyboard, no data jack. Only a metal call bell, old-fashioned, like something out of a classic Earth film.

Marcus bent over for a closer look. Given that the mining stations were manufactured on the Moon, it wasn't unusual to find terrestrial relics aboard. They were always small, something sentimental or prewar passed down from the prior generation: a decorative mug, pressed flowers. Once he had encountered an elegantly framed "cheese single" that still looked brand new. But this object seemed less ornamental and more... intentional.

Reaching out his right hand, he tapped the bell.

The server racks flickered off as one, followed by a dimming of the "overhead" lamps. The background hum of the station shifted, its pulse quickening.

He fell back a step, then stopped as his visor fogged over. Not the inside, but the outside, growing hazy like the decontamination bay all over again. He wiped at it, but the effect remained, the air itself seeming to thicken. Just as he was about to push it up, the servers flashed back on, banks of green scattering into pink and purple through the veil.

Marcus blinked to clear his vision.

Someone was sitting in the chair. Or *something*.

A hologram. Its edges congealed out of the aerosol mist. Faceless, gray, of indeterminate shape or sex, its gangly arms resting on the desk.

"Welcome, Assessor," it said, though it had no mouth with which to speak. "Please connect to the wireless network to proceed."

Marcus recoiled. A warning tone sounded from his helmet speakers, plus a glaring red alert at the top of his HUD:

INTRUSION DETECTED
FIREWALL ACTIVE

It was a blank: an AI-controlled simulacrum, designed to fulfill every human function—and desire. They had been banned for decades.

It glitched as they stared at each other, trying and failing to assume a pleasing shape in the absence of a data set. Revulsion wormed through his chest as the abomination probed his suit. He tried to think of the proper infraction code but was too distracted.

"Where—" he croaked, wincing. He sounded like the pilot. Clearing the gravel from his throat, he continued, "Where is Administrator Marshall?"

"Your experience will improve by connecting to the network," it said, a hint of irritation in its silken voice.

Marcus glanced at his HUD. The alert was still present but no longer flashing. He was secure. "Absolutely not," he said.

Its arms lengthened, stretching past the bell to the edge of the desk. Six long fingers extended from each malformed hand.

Marcus drummed at his terminal, navigating through a shortcut to his emergency manual. A lengthy index popped up, which he scanned with practiced precision.

OVERRIDE CODES

He hit OK and read out the number, "Compliance override

code 22643242, illegal use of processing power to simulate a human being."

The hologram stilled. When it spoke again, its voice was free of inflection, assuming the proper monotone one would expect from a computer. "Override accepted."

Marcus breathed a sigh of relief, blinking away the nervous sweat that trickled from his brow. "Where is Administrator Marshall?"

"Administrator Marshall is currently off-site."

"Off-site?"

"Hab Pod D-8 has been selected for your stay."

He shook his head. "Off-site where?"

"Administrator Marshall is currently off-site."

"You already said that."

"Hab Pod D-8 has been selected for your stay."

The blank had regressed all the way into binary stupidity.

"Fine," he grumbled. "When will she be back?"

"Unknown."

"Unknown?"

"Unknown."

Marcus clenched his fists. Aggravation and adrenaline buzzed along his nerves. "Disengage," he snapped.

The blank sizzled but remained coherent.

"Disengage," he repeated, less confident this time.

Its head ballooned, skin tone fluctuating until it resembled something almost human. A pixel-thin line emerged where lips should be. Two dark pools formed into eyes, sucking in the surrounding light, staring at him, into him.

Marcus stumbled, dragging his focus back to his HUD even as his body drifted forward, toward the creature. He needed an emergency shutdown code. He tore through the document index, fingers twitching at the controls. Just as he found it, the hologram shuddered, its strange mouth working as it clipped out a final farewell.

"Have a—good—day, Aaaaaaa-ssessor."

It dissipated with a sigh. The server racks returned to their prior jumble of colors. The station quieted.

Marcus straightened his posture, wincing at the pops in his neck. His heart was racing. Missing a scheduled appointment with an official representative of the empire was one thing. Substituting an abomination was entirely another. Distance was no excuse; Psyche Station was bound by the same laws as Mars.

He backtracked from the current menu, bringing up his draft assessment, and tapped the dictation button. "Note infrac—" His voice gave out, absent enough breath. Blood pounded in his ears.

Navigating to the station schematic instead, he toggled on the legend, then zoomed into the habitat ring until he found his assigned pod. He could work on his assessment later, once he was settled, then find out where the administrator—or anyone on this cursed station—was hiding. Allowing a few moments to recover, with a glance or two at the chair to make sure it was still unoccupied, he snatched up his suitcase and made his way forward.

Beyond Central Receiving, a steel-railed catwalk ran a few meters ahead before branching along the inner curve of the hub toward the station's four transit spokes. The layout was the same as every other station he'd visited: spokes set clockwise from A to D, joined at the center by a bulky junction of riveted steel and exposed lift gears. Habitation pods lined the "top" half of the ring, communal facilities in the other.

Spoke C lay directly ahead. Spoke A hung above it like some sort of nocturnal predator. The remaining two spokes jutted from the walls on either side, though the left-hand spoke

—Spoke D, the one he was meant to take—was blocked by a construction barrier, its elevator disassembled into parts.

Marcus checked behind him, scanning the still-hazy air around the receiving desk, then made for the right-hand spoke.

The ceiling lift was technically closer to his destination, but the thought of walking up there sent a shudder through his bowels. This way he only had to walk sideways rather than upside down. The disorientation got even worse at the end of the spokes, where the outer wall of the habitat ring became the floor no matter which lift you took. Up and down meant nothing in space.

The handrail was the only constant, squealing under his augmented grip until he reached the shaft. A wire-mesh lift waited at the top, in only marginally better shape than its broken-down counterpart, stripped of most of its paint and bruised with corrosion. The gnarled edge of its metal floor plates curled over a gap just wide enough to ensnare his booted feet. Gaping alongside the lift was an open pit lined with an emergency ladder.

He peered over the edge, seriously considering the manual route, but there was too much darkness below. Thrusting his suitcase forward, he grasped both sides of the cage and high-stepped inside, setting each boot down gingerly so as not to dislodge anything. There was no door to close, only two buttons: Up and Down.

Bracing himself, Marcus pressed Down.

# 5

# HABITAT RING

The lift shuddered as it ground its way down the spoke, scrapes and bangs echoing all around him, growing louder as the junction faded away. Shadow claimed the floor of the cage first, then his legs, then his arms. Just as darkness threatened to swallow him entirely, a single jittering lamp came to life on the wall beside the emergency ladder. Then another as the first fizzled out, illuminating only a few rungs, the pattern repeating as he descended into the habitat ring.

It wasn't long before the pull of artificial gravity dragged at his body, an uncomfortable pressure building in his knees. His spine compressed. Organs shifted. Blood settled independently of his compression layer's coaxing, filling his legs until it seemed his mag boots were on overdrive. Between each strobe of light from the shaft, his suitcase crept closer to the floor, canting sideways against the station's rotation.

By the time the lift emerged into the habitat ring, screeching to a halt against its guiderails, Marcus felt like a bug crushed underfoot. Rotational gravity was an imperfect science: simulating 1 G required either an enormous ring or velocities that left inhabitants with the spins. The relatively small mining stations managed less than half that, roughly Mars-standard, which suited him fine. It was all he had ever known. Still, he couldn't shake the feeling of being flung about in space, his guts lagging behind the rest of his body.

A bio-monitor flashed on his HUD, but he dismissed it with a swat at his terminal. There were already too many competing compounds circulating through his veins. Instead, he brought up the local map again, locating the tiny pod that would serve as his home on Psyche Station. Given his current state, he was glad to be unaccompanied for the journey.

Stepping into the access corridor, he proceeded anti-spinward, slowly at first as he found his footing and as motion sensor lights flickered on in his presence. The habitat ring was no less grubby than the lift, with peeling white paint, stains, and even rivulets of moisture winding across the walls. He considered opening his visor to test the air, then remembered Themis Station's eye-watering aroma and kept it shut.

The passage felt especially narrow absent portholes to gaze through, highways of pipe and conduit pressing close against his helmet. Bulkheads protruded at odd intervals, their edges catching his suitcase, now an anchor, as he kept drifting to the right.

Eventually, he'd learn to compensate for the Coriolis effect. At least until he returned to the hub to track down the station's delinquent administrator. After which he'd have to adapt all over again, and again. His knees hurt just thinking about it. As mundane as the shuttle rides were, at least they were consistent. He had grown accustomed to floating through the void, to the effortlessness of microgravity.

Hab door numbers blurred past as he reminisced, occasionally checking the mini-map pinned to his HUD. No other lights came on downtunnel. No harried workers rushed past to return to their duties. So far, the ring was as empty as the hub. Likewise, his footsteps were more muted than usual, as though walking underwater.

Marcus was exhausted by the time he reached the landing for Spoke A—no longer upside down—then his pod two units farther on. Fatigue gnawed at his thinned-out bones, despite the long sleep in transit. It always went that way; drug-induced unconsciousness rarely translated into restfulness.

An ocular sensor waited below his door number, a red LED indicating the room was locked. He hadn't noticed if the ones he had passed were red or green. Craning over with a grunt, he forced his eyes wide and pressed the Scan button. The interior of his helmet flared blue, followed by an angry buzz from the pad. He wiped the front of his visor, stuck out his neck until his eyelashes grazed the glass, and tried again to no effect. Reluctantly, he pushed the visor up and away, though mindful enough to hold his breath. Even still, the sharp tang of mold clawed at his nostrils. He pressed the button a third time, wincing as he was temporarily blinded. The pad chattered to itself, digesting his identity, then clicked to green.

He slammed the visor back down, huffed in a breath of air as his climate control recirculated, and pushed on the panel. The door slid into the wall and an interior light blinked on, revealing a rectangular module only slightly larger than his accommodations on the shuttle. He hurried inside, tapping the door closed behind him.

Like the corridor, the room was windowless and cramped. An oversized air vent jutted from the ceiling, as if to reassure the occupant they wouldn't suffocate in their sleep. The adjacent LED lamp waffled between dim and dimmer. Much of the room was taken up by the bed: a proper one at least, not just a recliner, fitted with actual sheets and a thin gray comforter. Marcus lingered on the inviting curves of the half-covered pillow, eyes drooping, sleep tugging at him—and the dreams that waited there.

Sighing, he checked the time: 11:50.

Still six hours until bed if he wanted to reset his sleep cycle. Six hours to kill. He caught himself, a guilty flush warming his cheeks. Six hours to do his job, rather.

He set down his case and took in the rest of the room. There wasn't much to see. A pair of lockers at the end of the bed, a fold-down desk at the head, and a small work chair rounded out the furnishings. Around the bulkhead from the front door was a cubby with a steel toilet and sink. Showers were communal, in facilities located all the way back by Spokes B and D.

Six hours... then one more day after that and he'd be done. On his way back home. Not that his apartment was much more glamorous than this, but it was his. Working at his own desk, sleeping in his own bed, without worrying as much about what lurked on the other side of the walls. It all seemed so fuzzy now, like a half-remembered vid.

He stared down at his suitcase, considering its contents and a decision he had to make: whether to remove his exosuit for his stay. He hadn't on Ceres Station. It was a second skin by then. Same with Hygiea.

He frowned—was that right?

Was his helmet off on Themis or did he just have his visor up?

It wasn't just his life on Mars that seemed distant. Everything before his shuttle ride to Psyche Station was mired in fog, vague silhouettes that slipped farther away the harder he tried to remember. The compounding effects of drugs and sleep deprivation.

He eyed the door, imagining the dank corridor beyond. The reek of poorly scrubbed air. Radioactive particulates blowing about, tracked in by the peculiar workers Ceres Station's administrator had warned him of.

"It's not right over there," the man had said, eyes wide, voice trembling.

That was a given. It wasn't right anywhere. Not this far out.

No, he would keep the suit on. But he did have to clean it. Protocol demanded that much. Though his memory was addled, all procedures regarding the OSSM Mk I Combat Exosuit were etched deeply into his brain. The military consultant back home had made sure of that.

Marcus knelt and thumbed open his case, inching backward as its internal mechanisms whirred to life. A series of snaps and beeps sounded before the lid yawned open, disgorging an array of tiered compartments. Dozens of trays slid up and out, more than should fit in such a small space. Each was customized to its contents, tidy, perfect, arranged in order of the maintenance schedule: sanitization up top; consumables in the middle; fuel cells and filter cartridges below. A negligible portion at the very bottom was reserved for his own personal effects.

The exosuit was worth more than he was; both the OSSM trainer and his director had made that abundantly clear. To wear it was an honor and a privilege, and it needed to be returned in the same condition it was issued. He had been resentful at first. The cumbersome frame seemed like overkill, intensely claustrophobic. But the longer he wore it, the more he appreciated its myriad capabilities, especially the servo augmentation. Like many of his generation, he had been born frail, especially so, with a physiology poorly adapted even to Mars's mild gravity. The armor negated that weakness, to the point where he had become dependent on it. Giving it back was the only part of going home he dreaded.

Taking a deep breath, he pulled the release latch on his collar. His eardrums fluttered as the suit's climate control spun down, then popped as he removed his helmet. The overhead air vent hummed in greeting. All around him, the station came alive with the noisome complaint of its rotation. Alternating rattles and creaks echoed from the corners of the room, which grew larger and darker without the constant stream of telemetry from his heads up display. It was like losing a sense. Reluctantly, he set the helmet on the bed, doffed his gloves, and set to work.

The process was laborious but not unwelcome, the physicality of it a relief from his increasingly wandering thoughts. He followed the steps exactly, removing one section of armor at a time to the lockers, bed, and floor; inspecting fasteners for wear; lubricating joints; detaching sensors, injectors, and reams of medical and data cable; and sanitizing every skin-contact point with a robust chemical spray that made his eyes water. The bulky cuirass came last, housing most of the combat suit's mechanical and computer systems. Getting it off required an awkward feat of contortionism, followed by a diagnostic sequence that took longer than all the other parts combined.

Finally, Marcus stood within a gleaming circle of shed skin, stripped down to his compression layer. There was hardly space to move. Had he been following protocols to the letter, the exosuit would have been broken down and stowed in the hub's decontamination bay. But given the circumstances, this was an acceptable deviation.

He rolled his shoulders, stretched his gangly arms and legs, and once again considered the option of showering. His undergarments were designed to mitigate bacteria, particularly the diaper-like shell encasing his privates, but technology could only hold back entropy for so long.

In short, he could smell himself.

Instinctively, he reached for his detached wrist terminal to bring up the map, then stopped. He didn't need it. He knew where the showers were: a long way back.

Instead, he unzipped his compression layer, peeling it down to his boots but not off completely. The room wasn't cold—if anything, it was unusually warm and humid—but he shivered nonetheless. He sprayed himself with the same disinfectant used on the armor, careful to avoid the bruised valleys of flesh around his medical ports. The wan skin brightened on contact, almost assuming a human tone. Biting back the chemical sting, he wiped off the residue with a cloth, then applied the remainder to his girdle and undergarments. By the time he was done, the room was glowing, air exchangers struggling to clear the vaguely mint-scented fog.

Hiking up his pants halfway, he waddled over to the toilet and winced as his raw buttocks met the seat—quite cold this time. An ailing electric motor chugged to life, followed by the sudden pull of vacuum. He tried to relax, even while gripping a handhold to resist being sucked into the station's subterranean depths. When he was done, a woefully brief mist sprayed his privates, followed by a blast of air. The motor crumped off as he wobbled upright and out of the cubby.

Marcus sighed. Maybe shitting into the suit wasn't so bad after all.

He zipped himself up and found his wrist terminal on the bed. The chronometer on its microdisplay read 13:22.

An hour and a half had passed. If he settled for just wearing his mag boots, he could get in a solid four hours of work. An unexpected gurgle echoed from his stomach—and maybe he could have a proper meal.

The air vent cycled down, allowing the other sounds of the room to creep back in. But there was something else now: a dull, rhythmic thump from the access corridor, getting louder as it approached his pod.

Marcus stiffened.

The administrator? Come to apologize?

His gaze flicked around the room at the mess he'd made, then down at himself. Mag boots and fancy undergarments painted a poor picture of an imperial assessor on official business. He tugged at the skintight fabric, but it made little difference. At least it was clean.

The thumping stopped outside his door.

He sniffed once, wrinkling his nose at the mélange of competing aromas in his module. Hopefully she wouldn't notice, given the station's general condition.

He eyed the control pad, still waiting for a doorbell chime. Or a knock.

Neither came.

Marcus adjusted his compression layer again, but this time his hands were trembling. He wished for his heads up display, hated not knowing exactly how much time had passed, hated how vulnerable he was. His gaze lingered on the door, as though he could see through to the other side.

Still nothing.

A stream of excuses rushed into his mind: not footsteps but structural settling, or station-keeping thrusters.

It didn't matter. Decision made, he set about putting his exosuit back on. With haste.

Fifteen minutes later, he was ready for duty. Fully charged and minty fresh, he rested a hand on the control pad, listening to the station's creaking for a moment before opening it and stepping back out into the habitat ring.

It was empty.

Good.

Better to interrogate the crew on his terms. He brought up the mini-map. Both the mess hall and operations module lay back the way he'd come, on the other side of Spoke B. Double-checking that his pod had auto locked, he headed out.

# 6
# PAVLOVA

The ceiling lights sputtered to life as though resentful of being woken again so soon, casting just enough illumination to navigate the corridor's perpetual curve. Even so, Marcus had to trail a hand along the wall for balance. It wasn't just the dim that threw him off, but direction—spinward rather than anti-spinward. The walk to his pod had felt like a descent. This time gravity tugged at him in fits. Repeated twiddling of his mag boot settings didn't help, so he focused on the other hab modules instead.

Every door he passed was marked by a red light. And silence. The quiet should have been a comfort, but it only amplified the station's background chatter, transforming hisses and ticks into conspiratorial whispers. He hurried past the last of them, finding relief as he reached the transit lift, still parked at the bottom.

Section B was next. After personnel interviews, it represented the mainstay of his work. Logs to parse, data to filter, and ultimately recommendations to produce. Exactly his skill set, rote work even. Yet when he continued down the corridor, it was with a sluggish step, the weight of expectation and responsibility pressing harder on him than the station's rotation ever could.

B-1, Sanitation, came up first, and with it a wave of itchiness across his arms and legs. The disinfectant had done its job, but at a cost.

He stopped for a moment to scratch uselessly at his armored thighs, only to notice the deck plating here was darker than the rest. Tapping on his helmet light, he traced the grime back toward the transit spoke. A definite trail ran between the lift and the showers, unnoticed when he had entered the habitat ring. The pattern was irregular, but not random, not just water stains or rust. Ovoid silhouettes extended from a sticky center, splaying out in every direction.

Footprints.

A few bore the geometric stamp of mag boots, but others were narrow, terminating in long toes joined by webs of muck. As though the crew had been scampering barefoot on the blackened walls of the hub. Or beyond...

Marcus shuddered, fragments of his dreams surfacing in the filthy mosaic. Green shimmers, sparkling gold dust, crusty floor seams widening into bottomless fissures. He blinked away the vision, grasping onto protocol instead.

"Note infraction," he muttered, before realizing he hadn't tapped the dictation button. He would do it later. Or get some answers from Administrator Marshall on what sort of unorthodox operation she was running here.

Pressing himself to the corridor wall, he edged past the worst of it and moved on. The floor soon resumed its normal level of grime. He flicked off his helmet light and picked up his pace.

B-2, Medical, was next; he would check there later. The last thing he needed in this moment was to pore over accident records, to see whatever was hidden inside the black-eyed crew's gangly bodies. He cleared his throat—and his mind—and kept moving.

The farther he traveled through Section B, the better its condition, as though it had barely been used. The walls were still mostly white. Lights shone a little brighter. By the time he reached B-3, Mess, his nerves had finally steadied. Leaning close to the door, he tapped up his input gain. The station's beating heart thundered in his ears, but there was no chatter on the other side, malevolent or otherwise. He reset his terminal and pressed the control pad.

The doors slid open without fanfare, flickering lights revealing what looked like... a storage room?

"What," he exclaimed, to no one in particular.

Stacks of gray plastic crates formed pillars to either side of the entrance, towering nearly to the ceiling. Beyond them, shorter stacks continued inward like crenelated walls around the room's two steel tables.

He double-checked the module number against his mini-map: B-3 was definitely the mess hall. The storage bays were farther downtunnel on either side of Spoke C.

The opening was barely wide enough for him. He squeezed through, pauldrons scraping as he passed. The left-hand pillar teetered, setting his stomach sideways, but stayed put. By the look of the crates, they were Mars-standard freight. One of the tables was completely surrounded, chairs relocated on top, while the other barely had room to sit. The galley peeked out from the back of the module, at the end of a narrow channel.

Tapping on his helmet's active scanning mode, he targeted the closest shipping label. A bounding box appeared on his HUD, followed by a blinking cursor as his suit computer located the log file. A few seconds later, a month-old text entry popped up listing various foodstuffs shipped from Mars in exchange for ore delivery. That was the system: ore out, food and other essentials in. No scheduled supply runs, just a balanced ledger. It had kept the mining crews in check for decades.

A steady stream of entries filled his visor as he weaved his way to the back of the module, scanning crates along the way. The dates grew older the farther he went, the oldest of them from several years ago.

It didn't make any sense. If Administrator Marshall's operation was under quota, they should have been hungry for supplies—and hungry in general. An infraction needed to be filed in any case.

He swapped out his scan for audio-visual dictation and panned around the room to capture video evidence. "Log infractions," he began. The Document icon on his HUD swelled in response, ready to transcribe. "One: Misuse of crew modules for storage. Two: Misappropriation of imperial resources. Attach scans and associated shipping logs as evidence. Also recommend full audit of Mars-receiving office for Psyche Station."

His list of questions for the administrator was piling as high as the crates. He added one more entry, "Add action item to check Medical for records of malnutrition among crew."

He disengaged the recording and continued to the galley.

It had been days since he'd eaten anything. Even so, and despite the presence of more food than anyone on Mars had ever seen at one time, his stomach emitted only a mild rumble. The kitchen, such as it was, consisted of a short counter fitted with a microwave, sink, faucet, and pull-out waterspout, above which hung the food cabinets. A dejected-looking coffee maker huddled in the corner never to be used again, not while Mars and its satellites remained cut off from Earth.

Marcus tested the spout with a quick tug on the handle. Nothing. He held it open longer, prompting a violent shudder from the plumbing stack and a trickle of brackish fluid. He counted down five seconds, the limit for open water on a space station. The flow increased somewhat, but its viscosity didn't change. He held it a few more useless seconds, breaching protocol, then shut it off. No surprise that the plumbing was in as bad shape as the rest of Psyche Station. He'd have to rely on his filters.

Connecting the dripping tube to his throat port, he turned on the water again. Tiny onboard motors whirred as his suit slurped it down, refilling hydration bags and reconstituting various life-sustaining solutions for later use. He was accustomed to the procedure by now, but the slow tap dragged it out, with nothing to do but stare at his own twisted reflection in the steel backsplash: a hulking machine-man latched to the counter with its mouthparts, lapping up nutrients like some kind of robotic fly.

After several minutes, the motors spun down and a full meter displayed on his HUD. He shut the tap and disengaged the spout, gagging reflexively as though removing it from his own throat, then slotted it back into its housing. Tapping on his terminal, he extended his helmet's hydration tube and took a test sip. It was fine for the most part, a little musty, chalky even, but enough to stir up his appetite.

Stomach now growling, he opened the first cabinet—and sighed in disappointment. Another infraction had been queued up and ready to go for possession of contraband substances, something resembling actual food. Instead, compliant rows of nutritional paste packets stared back at him, brightly color-coded to their various artificial flavors. On the shelf above were boxes of crackers, solid but bland, formulated more for dental health than taste; eating nothing but liquified food tended to make one's teeth fall out, like sailors of old.

He tried the other cabinets, but they presented more of the same. There were, however, several old favorites he hadn't seen since childhood: prawn cocktail, turkey dinner, pavlova.

Enough variety to make a three-course meal of deconstructed soy protein and synthetic compounds. And their age didn't matter. Like that cheese single of old, paste had no official expiry date.

He flipped up his visor as though to allow his nose to guide him, but there was only the station's trademark metallic must. Grabbing a steel tray from under the sink, a package of turkey dinner, and a box of crackers, he cobbled together a trio of tiny sandwiches, beige all the way through. They looked and smelled distressingly like the contents of his girdle.

Turning about, he considered bringing his paltry meal to the one available table, but it would be pointless. Unlike the recliner in the shuttle, the flimsy dining chairs wouldn't hold his weight even in half-g; a problem he'd have throughout his stay, as long as he kept his suit on. Also, eating alone at the center of the towering labyrinth seemed far worse than just getting it over with.

He returned to his tray, gloved hands hovering at either side. They felt detached, as they had upon waking from his drug-induced slumber, in no hurry to shed their protective armor or to deliver the bleak payload to his gullet. The tray shimmered on the counter, catching fluctuations from the overhead lighting. Sparkling, like the stars that spun around him as the shuttle docked. As Psyche Station spun endlessly in space, its jagged shadow disappearing into the asteroid below—

Marcus coughed as a splash of stomach acid hit his esophagus.

His hands came back online, shuffling the tray's contents directly into the galley's disposal. Whirring blades and suction tubes shrieked as the remains were consumed on his behalf.

He would eat later.

Dropping his visor back down, he retreated from the mess hall and back into the corridor. The original plan was to proceed directly to the operations module, but the illegal supply situation warranted an inspection of the storage facilities first.

He checked the time—14:45—and blinked in confusion.

An hour since he left his pod.

He turned back to the still-open mess hall, wondering where the time had gone. How long had he stood there staring at his uneaten food?

No, he must have read his chronometer wrong the first time.

He palmed the doors shut and kept moving.

B-4, Operations, came up first, but he marched right past it, trying to restrain his runaway rumination. Solitude had that effect. Absent company, his mind made its own conversation. He was eager to speak with Administrator Marshall on official business, but it would also be nice to hear a voice other than his own rattling about in his head—assuming her vocabulary surpassed that of the pilot.

A dozen wandering trains of thought had been shut down by the time he reached B-5, the final module in the quadrant and the first storage unit. He opened the doors without hesitation.

The unit was full. Not just cluttered like the mess hall, but packed solid with crates. More freight from Mars, some so old that their labels had yellowed. Little light penetrated from above, and less still bled through gaps in the front row. There were only shadows on the other side, broken by an intermittent sparkle of reflected light and a faint clinking sound, as though something tethered had come loose.

Marcus appraised the stacks, looking for a spot where he could leverage his servo-enhanced strength to make a peephole. But just as he reached out, the clinking stopped. The sparkles coalesced into two white ovals smoldering in the dark, cycling in and out of existence as his visor tried and failed to compensate. He blinked hard, trying to exorcise the afterimages, but they wouldn't budge. Probably a reflection, like the spacesuit in the shuttle's docking compartment. Except every nerve ending in his outstretched arms was on fire and his airways were swelling shut.

He backed up a step, anxious to move on, when a different sound rose from the back of the module. Not mechanical this time, but not human either. A groan, low and piteous, raising every hair on his neck.

He fell back into the corridor, almost falling over entirely. One of the columns shifted, scraping the floor. Then the whole wall shuddered, bowing outward, threatening to burst free.

Instinct drove him to the control pad—or maybe the ghost of his combat suit. He slammed the door button, almost cracking it in two. The left side sealed immediately. The right side caught on the column, threatened to stall out, then continued along its track with a pained screech, closing just in time. A crash rang out from inside, followed by a cascade of heavy thuds against the steel slabs.

Marcus retreated all the way to the opposite wall, unsteady on his feet. But it wasn't just fear that imbalanced him. Even as the groan within the module was cut off, another arose, but this time it was the pained shifting of bulkheads.

A ripple ran across the floor joints. Everything rattled all at once. The station was wobbling, its rotation upset by too much mass shifting at once. A terse alarm blipped to life from a hidden speaker.

He found a handhold and latched on, breath held as he waited for the attitude thrusters to kick in. There were redundancies in place. This was minor, surely, compared to something like a docking misalignment. Though "less bad" in space still tended to be very bad.

Mercifully, it didn't take long.

Three tones replaced the alarm. A deep vibration coursed

through his armor into his bones, setting his knees straight again. The tones sounded a second time, then shut off as though nothing had happened.

The corridor remained empty.

He waited, peering left and right, but no one came running. Truly, nothing would rouse this crew from their hiding places. At least the automated systems were still operational.

He detached himself from the wall one vertebra at a time. Breathing heavily, repeatedly, until he could feel his lungs actually expand. The storage module was quiet and the indicator light on the control pad had switched to amber, indicating a fault. Getting the doors open again would be a challenge, not that he wanted to. His skin was still tingling, a slick of sweat at the back of his neck. Better that it was shuttered. Even if the groan had probably been mechanical.

Probably...

Logic crept back as his oxygen levels increased. Inventories from prior station audits scrolled through his memory. All the miscellanea that had been stuffed into nooks and crannies after decades in the void. He would know for sure when he reviewed the logs in Operations and could see what else the crew had been hoarding.

In the meantime, he was required to investigate the second storage module.

After a few more breaths...

He lingered opposite the doors, eyes fixed on the control pad just in case it changed its mind. His right hand found the empty belt hoops at his waist, as though reaching for a sidearm. He had never inquired with the OSSM officer about a weapon to complement his combat suit, nor had one been offered. Given his physical condition, he doubted any nascent marksmanship expertise. Still, in retrospect, it felt like an omission.

After a final scan for crewmembers who would never show

up, he continued on his way. Spoke C came up first, empty, its transit lift still in the hub. He didn't linger. There had been enough excitement already without revisiting the abomination above.

Another amber light pulsed up ahead. He slowed, double checking the number plate on the door, just in case he had somehow been turned around: C-1, the second storage module. But it too was showing a fault. They shouldn't have been linked in any way.

He reached for his data jack to prepare an override, then stopped, caught between fear and logic as he listened for the uncanny sound from the other unit. Wondering if whatever was in there might also be in here. The corridor behind him was silent, but an uneven buzz floated from ahead. The ceiling lights hadn't illuminated as far downtunnel as usual, suggesting issues all the way to the broken lift. If there was a general fault, forcing entry before determining the cause was against protocol.

He lowered his wrist terminal. He had no choice but to skip this one.

Still, curiosity dragged him forward.

No more lamps flickered on in his presence, but those behind turned off as usual, leaving him in darkness. He fumbled his helmet light on, sending a narrow beam of white through the pitch. His visor was also equipped with a multispectral mode, but he'd had quite enough specters of late.

Eventually, he arrived at C-2: Recreation—and another amber indicator.

A deep unease crept up his spine as he panned his light over the dust-caked control pad. It hadn't been touched in ages.

This was more than an infraction.

Where Section B housed modules essential to the station's mining operation, Section C served its crew. Recreation, exercise facilities, the chapel—all essential for physical and mental wellbeing. Without those, this far out for so long, Psyche Station would go the way of Europa.

Marcus winced, the muscles at the base of his skull knotting up. As jumbled as his memories were, it was impossible to forget the vids of that maligned station's final days. Mars had suffered greatly by its loss.

The weight of responsibility bore down on him once more.

He checked his chronometer, stifling an inappropriate yawn. A tired chill settled into his bones. Time was running out before his brain shut down, no longer propped up by pharmaceuticals.

He had to find out what was going on

He had to do his job.

# 7
# OPERATIONS

THERE WERE NO MORE surprises on the way back to Operations, just the steady echo of mag boots, quickening as he passed the storage unit, and the welcome buzz of working motion lights. Before long, Marcus was at his destination, untold hours of work on the other side. A familiar twinge of procrastination tugged him toward his wrist terminal.

The sudden need to check those ninety-three unread messages.

Not to mention the ragged state of his draft files.

He hadn't even checked filter integrity since refilling his water reservoirs in the mess hall.

Or run a compression test after reassembling his suit.

The doors opened. His hand was on the control pad, as though someone else had placed it there. He snapped it back and peeked inside.

The module appeared as it should for once. No crates piled up or other signs of disarray. Just an ordered grid of cubicles separated by a low barrier. Alternating server racks and cabinets ran the length of the double-shielded outer wall, making for tight quarters. It looked like his office back home.

The doors shut behind him as he made a beeline for the rearmost workstation, maintaining line of sight to the entrance.

Just in case.

It resembled Central Receiving: same cold metal desk, dual monitors, and an impractically narrow chair, which confirmed he'd be standing. A tremor rippled along his calves and a sigh across his chest. In retrospect, it might have been nice if the station's emergency systems hadn't kicked in earlier, if only for a few hours of zero-g. On the bright side, the desktops sported proper keyboards with data ports instead of call bells.

Finding a hand crank, he raised his desk to a usable height and tilted the monitors up. A tap on the keyboard brought up a login screen.

There was no more putting it off.

He extended his data jack, plugged it in, and waited as his suit interfaced with the server behind the screen. Somewhere behind him, a fan spun up. A zigzag of distortion ran across his visor, followed by an access prompt:

PSYCHE STATION OPERATIONS:
ASSESSOR ACCESS

He tapped the OK button on his terminal and waited as his suit delivered its master codes. Given the dire state of the station, he half-expected an authentication error, the crew hiding their tracks beneath a new encryption key. Part of him wished for it, so he'd be relegated to a raw data dump and an expedited trip home. Though even if they had blocked the way, the advanced processors on his suit would probably brute force it without him even knowing.

ACCESS GRANTED

So much for that.

DOWNLOADING LOGS TO SUIT STORAGE

The monitors crackled to life, multifold windows emerging from a primordial soup of green pixels. Dozens of them, self-arranging into status dashboards for every system on the station, every drone, and the mining site on the other side of 16 Psyche. Spreadsheets crammed with gradient-coded numbers. Waveforms juddering with deep space noise. And an endless scroll of call and response between the station and its satellites. Every data point he could ever want.

Except the figures were unreadable. There were too many, too small.

A dull ache bloomed at the center of his forehead. For all the exosuit's gifts, it had rendered him myopic, maladapted to reading anything beyond the horizon of his visor. Refocusing on his HUD, he found the download progress bar: it had barely moved. He was here for the long haul, shackled to the desk by his data jack. For now, he'd have to operate the old-fashioned way.

Taking a final huff of purified air, he pushed his visor up, blinking away the sudden influx of dust and the unfiltered glare of the screens. He gave the desk another couple cranks to bring the keyboard within typing range, grateful that he couldn't zoom into the grime between its ancient keys. Even so, he took his time removing his gloves.

It was slow going at first, but muscle memory took over even as his brain lagged. His long gray fingers flew over the keyboard, anxious to dismiss the dashboard view, which was no more readable even with his face pressed close. He selected the new Assessor Menu from the nav bar and disabled screen mirroring. The right-hand screen faded back into a greenish haze. The left simplified into a single, narrow interface, as close to his heads up display as possible.

There was a protocol to follow: local operations first, mining, then shipping.

He tabbed down to Live Map and hit ENTER, summoning a simplified 3D wireframe of the station: hub, spokes, and habitat ring. A legend near the bottom of the screen offered display toggles for every onboard system. He selected All, and a webwork of lines unfurled one by one, mapping out Psyche Station's circulatory and nervous systems. They filled every bulkhead until it was impossible to discern conduit from corridor from wall panel—except for a large black spot on the habitat ring.

A dead zone.

Marcus spun the station about one keystroke at a time until the void was front and center, then zoomed in. It was Section C, where he had just been. There were barely any lines active from the lift to the chapel, where they started to reappear. Electrical, plumbing, HVAC—all offline. And now that he had a tighter view of the ring, other malignancies appeared.

There were faults everywhere.

His ribs caught on the next breath, as though examining his own chest X-ray, riddled with cancer as every Martian's eventually was. He panned the diagram around until it centered on Operations, and the exact spot he was standing.

Every line was where it should be. His lungs refilled, though he was no less concerned for the station.

Returning to the menu, he selected System Logs. A wall of text filled the monitor, many of the timestamped lines bold and prefixed with an error tag. Too many.

He navigated to the query interface and filtered by unique errors detected in the last twenty-four hours. The wall shifted but was no less full. A counter at the bottom of the screen showed seventeen pages of results.

His calves twitched, anxious to run him all the way back to the shuttle.

Seventeen—that couldn't be right. And if it was, it was a wonder anything worked.

He flipped down his visor, just in case the bulkheads ruptured, or the walls electrified, or a gush of sewage flooded the deck. None of those things happened. Even so, he allowed himself a few high-pressure gulps of pristine oxygen before reopening his helmet.

He modified the time parameters to show active errors from a day ago, in case there had been an acute event prior to his arrival, or a temporary surge resulting from the rotation shift.

No change.

How long had it been this bad?

He reset the filters all the way back to the first day of operations and switched the output from log stream to visualization. The wall of text sizzled out, replaced by a graph showing faults on the y-axis, dates on the x. The server fans whirred a little louder as decades of data were crunched.

Slowly, a line emerged. It looked as it should at first: an oscillation, rising as faults accumulated and dipping back as they were addressed, plateauing occasionally when replacement parts had to be shipped from Mars. Normal, until the line advanced to three years ago, coinciding with the first shipping anomalies and the genesis of his journey here. From that point onward it only climbed. No dips. No repairs. As though no one could be bothered to do their job. Or the station had been abandoned.

*Administrator Marshall is currently off-site.*

So said the abomination, the only resident of the empty hub above. But what about the rest of the crew? They couldn't all be gone. The mining facility was mostly automated, not designed for long-term accommodation, just maintenance.

Marcus navigated back to the main menu, found the CCTV system, and piped it to the second monitor. A new grid appeared, presenting grainy images from around the station. Most of the habitat ring views were unlit clouds of shifting pixels, save for the pinprick that marked each pod door.

Locked in—or out?

He skimmed quickly past, but the hub cameras were just as useless, most of them obstructed by the detritus he had observed on his way in.

Switching back to the other monitor, he brought up the maintenance schedule from the menu. An empty window popped in below the graph: nothing scheduled.

"Nothing, nothing, nothing," he muttered, irritation curling his fingers into talons.

*Something* was definitely wrong, but it was impossible to identify the root cause at this point. The crew? The data itself? The station mainframe couldn't be trusted, not fully, given the artificial intelligence poisoning its circuits.

He had to speak to the administrator.

Backtracking all the way up the menu, he switched his data source from the station to the mining facility and requested both text logs and visualization. A fresh wall of text tumbled onto the screen.

No bold lines.

No error tags.

The graph below it was the inverse of the station's: problems evident early on, then a steady stream of repairs, dropping to near flawless operation at the point where local operations went sideways. A third window popped up reporting drone statuses: all operational. It should have been a relief, but the churning in his gut said otherwise.

What were they doing down there?

Clearly not the job they were supposed to, given the shipping shortfalls.

He switched to exterior cameras, but there was no video feed to see for himself. A dorsal camera on the station's antenna mast stared up at nothing, and the ventral camera on the docking ring was locked onto 16 Psyche's north pole. The sole moving object on the screen.

His hand hovered over the keyboard for a moment, then tapped once to expand the window.

The asteroid juddered toward the edges of the monitor, almost past it. Spinning in sync with the station, yet so slowly that it appeared to drift backward along with the few meager stars that haloed it. Stars, or drones, buzzing about the opposite side. Flashes of sunlight arced across its jagged surface, bands of color seeping from the monochrome screen: viridian and gold and rust as bright as blood.

The churning in his stomach turned to motion sickness. Marcus grasped the desk, sending the monitors wobbling, and shut his eyes against the glare. But the afterimage persisted: 16 Psyche throbbing in the dark, as though alive

He snapped down his visor and found the download status bar: 42% and crawling ever so slowly to completion. Once it finished, he could run some sanctioned algorithms, in case he was missing something obvious. In the meantime, there was nothing to do but watch and wait.

He replaced his gloves and straightened, settled somewhat by the clean, metered air slipping into his lungs. Breathing deeply, he worked his terminal and piped the live camera feed into his helmet. 16 Psyche reappeared on his HUD, rotating in slow, manageable frames. If he couldn't get answers from the administrator, he'd have to go there himself. He had no choice. This was a costly mission; his superiors had drilled that into him. A one-off born of necessity. Returning without positively identifying, and resolving, the issues at hand was not an option.

43%.

A long blink stole the next few seconds.

44%.

He watched, even as fatigue pulled at his eyelids.

And waited.

# 8
# SAFE HARBOR

*The once-man floats over the surface of the asteroid. Cheeks puffed out, lips pressed shut, spindly arms and legs blowing in the cosmic breeze. Naked, wrapped in the black velvet of the void.*

*Before him looms a giant door carved from the mountainside. It has neither seams nor handles nor any mark of manufacture, yet he knows it to be such. A muffled call beckons from within, unceasing since the dawn of time. Chanting, many voices combined into a subsonic thrum. Awaiting a response, a command that will open the way.*

*The once-man strains to understand the words but they are too old, too terrible. He must only repeat them, open his throat to the vacuum. But the once-man was too recently a man. Fear shutters his mouth and petrifies his flesh.*

*Unable to speak, he beats upon the door, shattering his arms.*

*The call comes again.*

*He kicks the door until his legs crumble to dust.*

*The way remains shut. The chant dissipates into noise, the background chatter of the void. Blipping on and off as he spins in darkness.*

*Forever cast out.*

Marcus opened his eyes.

An alarm tone was ringing in his helmet. High pitched, buzzing in his teeth as much as his ears. On and off, on and off.

Glowing shapes materialized in the dim. 05:00 pulsed at the top of his HUD next to a completed progress bar. And a window, black on black: the camera feed, still running, though he couldn't make anything out. Just digital noise, obstructed by a string of drool from his open mouth, as though he were prone. He swallowed it back.

The chronometer ticked over to 05:01, and the alarm sequence restarted.

He tried to reach for his terminal, but his arm was stuck.

"What..."

He tried again, but it didn't move. Pinned, maybe. The other arm was also stuck, and his legs wouldn't budge. Only his heart rate monitor was moving freely, ticking up along with the thumping in his chest.

Bearing down, he strained to shift any part of his body, but it was useless. He was completely immobile. Limbless, like in the fading dream.

Another shape emerged on his HUD, a sequence of letters pulsing in tandem with his exertions:

`SENTRY MODE ACTIVE`

"Sentry mode," he blurted, speaking aloud to combat his rising panic.

There were so many modes and functions and statuses to remember, prattled off one after the other by the OSSM officer, but the fog of sleep was too thick.

Instead, he peered past the clutter on his visor. A monitor bezel surfaced through one gap, a keyboard in another—the workstation. He was still in the cubicle, not lying down but bent over as though hanging from a tether. He craned his head around in his helmet. His arms were locked at his sides, data jack stretched taut from his wrist terminal. He must have fallen asleep standing up.

Sentry mode...

The suit knew somehow, via breathing patterns or heart rate or some kind of active monitoring he wasn't privy to, and instead of waking him, had gone rigid to keep him from tipping over. The same servos that once strengthened his feeble limbs now shackled them in place.

Too smart. Too independent. Too much like the blank.

The alarm blared again, clawing at his nerves.

"Disengage," he commanded through clenched teeth.

Nothing happened.

He collected himself, breathed deeply through his nose. Specificity mattered.

"Disengage Sentry Mode."

The alert vanished. The suit whirred and clicked as its servo brakes released, dropping him free. He caught the desk just in time, but it groaned under his weight. One of the legs buckled, sending the right-hand monitor from its perch. He grabbed it before it could fall, crushing the frame in his fist. The CCTV feed crackled and died.

05:02. The alarm sounded again.

He steadied himself, waited a moment in case anything else was about to collapse, then stabbed at his terminal to shut off the screeching.

Merciful silence.

But for the first time, Marcus felt like a passenger inside his own suit. He could set alarms and other sundry functions, but its autonomic systems were its own. Untouchable.

He articulated each joint in turn—wrists, elbows, knees—just to be sure everything was back to normal, for now at least.

Continuing to breathe as the adrenaline cleared from his bloodstream. The drugs would take longer, evidenced by the involuntary twitches along his fingertips and the jabbing behind his eyes. Sleep should have helped, but being strung up like a marionette all night certainly hadn't.

He tapped on his terminal menu, debating another dose—something to take the edge off—then opted for hydration instead. Today was too important, requiring all of his wits. He caught the tube in his mouth and drank heartily.

Before long, a dull pressure bloomed in his abdomen. He let go his bladder with only a token wince of pride. The suit gurgled as drinking water sloshed up and urine sloshed down, only a thin membrane separating them.

Best not to think about it.

Eventually, the readouts on his HUD crisped back into shape. The edges of the camera feed straightened, but the picture still didn't look right. 16 Psyche was nowhere to be seen, only an ocean of shifting pixels.

He nudged the tube aside, squeezed a few more drops into his girdle, and brought up the camera IDs. The feed had switched from exterior to interior, the station hub specifically. Even so, it didn't match what he remembered from last night. New shapes obscured the bulkheads, long and thin, shifting from light green to dark. The resolution was terrible. There was no thermal or infrared option like his visor. He brought up a filter menu and punched up brightness and contrast.

Gangly silhouettes emerged from the darkness. Human silhouettes.

The crew.

They listed in zero-g, like rotten fruit hanging from a dead tree. Five of them, swaying within their netting, drab uniforms and equally drab skin blending into the walls. Even at full brightness, he couldn't make out their faces. He could only imagine their black saucer eyes, slit nostrils, and forked tongues —all the reports from Ceres magnified a hundredfold.

Had they been there the whole time, leering down at him as he marched from the airlock to Central Receiving?

No, he would have seen them.

A new shift then, returned from "off-site," though no one actually seemed to be working. They just huddled together as though whispering dark secrets. A staccato hiss crackled from his comms even though the feed had no audio. Probably signal interference, but the frequency and timing made his skin crawl.

He watched and waited, just as he had before falling asleep, imagining movement in the absence of any. A slow turn from one of the crew, then another as they noticed the camera pointing their way. Detaching from their cluster, one monstrous limb at a time. Clambering on all fours, tongues lashing, ready to propel themselves off webbed feet.

Marcus pulled out his data jack.

The feed lingered a second longer than it should have, then cut. His visor cleared. Only the chronometer, a collapsed nav menu, and the lingering download bar remained.

He stared at the bar, wondering if he could shirk his duties just this once. Retreat to his pod, wait for the shuttle, and go home. His suit had logged everything. He could copy and paste all seventeen pages of infractions, recommend a total crew swap, and call it a day. Assessment complete.

But the empire wasn't a corporation. Data alone wasn't enough. Personal involvement was mandatory. Direct interviews. Answers, not conjecture. A signed, witnessed action plan delivered to the administrator. If the crew was back, she may be too.

Protocol. There was no escaping it.

Or them.

He brought up his suit menu, hovering again over the pharmaceutical inventory. The edge was still very much there, sharpened by too little gravity and too many tall tales—psychosis by a thousand cuts. He drummed his fingers on his terminal arm, trying to summon a past version of himself. One who would scoff at such hysterics. The professional, chosen for good reason, trusted to root out fraud and inefficiencies whether in processes or people. But the empire was very far away. And the people out here were... different. Too long removed from society. More adapted to darkness than light.

His fingers continued to tap in long, languid strokes. He clenched his hand until they stilled, then navigated to the station map. Hub and ring popped up on his visor, a snapshot but presumably still accurate. Section C looked just as bad as before. The storage, recreation, and exercise modules were definitely offline, but the chapel seemed intact. He brought up a location submenu and found a service schedule: Morning Mass, 05:30.

Safe harbor.

Assuming the resident priest wasn't also off-site.

Marcus picked himself up and trudged out of Operations, motorized joints whining their accommodation. He paused at the doorway to consider his approach. Spinward lay the unlit, potentially hazardous halls of Section C. Anti-spinward were the hab modules and a possible encounter with more returned crew. Turning on his heel, he headed for Section C. At least there he knew the risks, and he could record additional evidentiary data along the way.

Just in case he lost his nerve after all.

As he reached the section's storage module, he tapped on audio-visual dictation and began his rundown.

"Now entering Section C. Storage module C-1 inaccessible, likely due to improper stowage."

No need to go into detail on the other storage module.

"Modules C-1 through C-3 showing widespread faults on system map. Suspect cascading electrical failure due to severe dereliction in maintenance. Sensor lights not responding past C-1. Doors inaccessible."

He walked ahead several meters, stopping beneath a silent air vent. "HVAC offline."

Another meter on, a line of rust curled up the wall to a bundle of sweating pipe. "Condensation on water line, suggesting possible over-pressure."

From this point was darkness.

Marcus flicked on his helmet light and continued downtunnel, methodically logging every faulty light bank, pipe, access panel, and door. Plus a host of environmental anomalies as reported by his suit's sensors: cabin pressure, temperature, humidity, and oxygen levels. All out of spec. More than enough evidence for a crew recall.

Each report filled him with a mix of satisfaction and dread, the sense that once his own derelict checklist was complete, the station would simply disintegrate. The farther he descended, the weaker his lights. Floor, ceiling, and walls fell away, leaving only a disembodied trail of viscera to examine. More than once, he thought he had been turned around, but it was just a repeating pattern of neglect.

To the right, another dead panel.

Above, another knocking pipe.

Below, more broken floor tiles.

To the left—

Something glinted in the distance: a shape that didn't belong, mounted to the wall. He extended his arms to avoid slamming into a bulkhead, inching forward until the shape resolved into a cross—a crucifix—no larger than his wrist terminal. Its edges glowed as though lit from within, untouched by the surrounding decay. The cross itself was golden brown, with dark, spiraling whorls—real wood. The figure of Jesus was silver, faint tool marks catching the light. Hand-worked.

This was no terrestrial bauble, but a proper artifact.

Panning to the right, he found an alphanumeric stamp: C-4. The chapel.

He had arrived faster than expected—the chronometer on his HUD blinked 05:26—or maybe later. Time had blurred along the way. And the lights were still out, despite what the system map had shown and his own private hopes. He waved an arm in the air, but the motion sensors ignored him. Tracing his way along the wall, he came to the module's sealed double doors. The control pad beside them was completely dead.

"Dammit," he muttered, then flushed with guilt as he realized his dictation was still running. A slap at his terminal shut it off. Remembering where he was, and the crucifix hanging nearby, he crossed himself for good measure.

He tapped at the control pad a couple times, but nothing happened. Running his helmet light to the floor, he found the emergency access panel hinged partly open. He knelt down and pried it the rest of the way, wincing as a pained squeak echoed down the corridor.

The manual override crank was gone.

"Who's there?" came a muffled call.

Marcus jolted.

The sound seemed to come from inside, but the doors were too thick for that. He glanced up at the control pad. Tucked between the ocular scanner and intercom grille was a small camera lens.

"Yes, I can see you," the voice continued. Male, hoarse, but not guttural like the pilot. With a slight, very un-Martian lilt.

Marcus stood slowly, arms out.

"OSSM?" the man asked.

Marcus eyed his empty breastplate. The flaming sword that

would normally adorn it had been swapped out for plain composite, but there was no mistaking a combat exosuit. "No—" he began, voice catching in his throat. He cleared it, so as not to sound like the crew he was avoiding. "No. Imperial Assessor, Marcus O."

No reply.

"I came for morning Mass," he added.

Something scraped along the bottom of the wall and the right-hand door popped open an inch. A rustle of fabric came through the crack, followed by an annoyed huff. "Turn that down, would you?"

Marcus blinked in confusion, then realized his helmet light was glaring straight through the opening. He dialed it back until only faint tracers remained.

A pair of beady eyes filled the gap. Brown, not black. Normal-sized. "Show me your eyes," the voice said.

Marcus flipped up his visor without thinking. Frankincense and stale wine flooded his nostrils, overpowering the corridor's background must.

The man squinted at him. "Assessor, you say?"

"Yes. From Mars."

"Indeed..."

"Here for Mass."

The man continued to stare, assessing the assessor.

"Are you..." Marcus trailed off, hit with another pang of guilt. He hadn't checked the chapel's personnel roster along with the schedule. "Are you the priest?"

The man pressed his face closer to the gap, eyes rolling from side to side.

Marcus followed his gaze down the corridor. There was only pitch. When he turned back, the gap was empty. Another round of noises emanated from inside, a chorus of grinding gears and the strained grunts of the man working the crank. The door juddered open with each turn, stopping halfway.

"Come on, then," the voice called.

There was barely room to squeeze through. A dull glow emanated from within, illuminating rows of empty steel chairs and a modest altar at the far end. No narthex or holy water font to greet him. No other congregants.

Marcus fought the urge to drop his visor back down, crossed himself a second time, and stepped inside.

# 9

# THE PRIEST'S TALE

The man, clearly the station priest, worked furiously to close the door. His green vestments and stole flapped about as he muttered to himself, the cloth dulled from long use. Marcus held back an offer of assistance even though his servo-enhanced arms would make short work of the job. It seemed a sacred ritual, not to be disturbed: the call of the crank, the response of whispered invocations.

Sweat beaded along the priest's brow, his bone-white hair glowing like a halo beneath a nearby LED candle. The chapel was full of them, guttering from the walls in the same preprogrammed cadence. Just enough to keep the shadows at bay. There were no other signs of power.

Another turn of the crank, another prayer.

The priest didn't look like the rest of the crew, or even like Marcus. A tinge of pink still colored his complexion, the kind left by years under an unfiltered sun. His nose was redder still from too much drink. Despite his age and apparent vice, he was robust: thick-boned, glimpses of taut muscle beneath his yellowed collar and cuffs.

Earth-raised.

The door squealed shut with an extra-long turn of the crank and a huffed "Amen." Satisfied, the priest ratcheted himself back to standing and banged a particular pattern on the control pad. Just as Marcus was about to intervene, it lit up.

"You have power?" he asked, confused.

An array of lights blinked out a boot sequence and a hazy view of the corridor appeared on the monitor.

"Yes," the priest mumbled, pressing close to the screen.

"But the pad was out on the other side."

"Yes."

The local grid must have been tampered with. A severe infraction. But why?

The priest said nothing more for a long stretch, engrossed in the view. Finally, he tapped off the monitor and turned, startling as though noticing Marcus for the first time. His hand came up to his chest, rubbing at the embroidered cross on his chasuble. The golden thread there had been worn down to little more than an outline.

"Father?" Marcus said, trying to break the silence.

The priest looked him up and down, his eyes the same color and intensity as the cross outside.

Though Marcus stood a head taller than the man, each scan brought a wave of self-conscious heat. He felt naked without his visor, fully exposed by that singular breach in his armor. Wan complexion and blackened eyes on display. Spindly beneath all that bulk.

Not unlike the crew.

"You can't trust the cameras," the priest said.

"No." It was all Marcus could think to say.

"It's good that you came."

Marcus eyed the closed doors. "Will no one else be coming?"

The priest didn't answer. Instead, he lurched forward, a practiced wince on his face as his left leg dragged behind him—an old injury from another time. He made the sign of the cross over Marcus then limped up the aisle, thumbing on low-smoke censers along the way. Soon, there was only the earthy musk of frankincense.

The altar was already set: a black leatherbound missal open and waiting, a single host on the silver paten. No chalice. The priest mumbled something about being out of wine, then crossed to the tabernacle and withdrew a second host.

Marcus's throat clenched at the sight of it, dry all at once. He clomped slowly over to the rearmost pew.

The priest turned his way, as if only then remembering the question. "They go outside to pray now," he said.

Before Marcus could respond, the priest returned to the altar and set the second host atop the first. His movements were slow, precise. Green vestments swirling in the dim like 16 Psyche below. Shimmering with captured light, bulging with each breath.

"*In nomine Patris*—" The priest paused, as if catching himself, then continued, "In the name of the Father, and of the Son, and of the Holy Spirit."

Realizing they were going right into the liturgy, Marcus hurriedly unlatched and removed his helmet. The seal resisted at first, biting at his skin before letting go with a wet, sucking sound.

"—confess to almighty God."

The words hit him like a gale. He stumbled back, almost dropping his helmet. Open air beat against his unprotected ears. The growing stench from the censers burned his nose and throat.

Marcus knew the prayer of confession, had spoken it enough times, but it was lost in this moment. Each time he tried to regain his thoughts, another overloaded sense pulled him away. Time sped and slowed, as it had in the corridor, then resumed all at once with a shout and the first blow of the priest's hand against his chest. Marcus flinched, as though his own chest had been struck.

"Through my fault," the priest repeated, now with a rasp as he thumped his chest a second time.

The third strike was so loud that it echoed through the chapel. "Through my most grievous fault." He wheezed through several breaths before continuing.

This time, Marcus followed along, but only in his head. The fear of half-remembered dreams held his mouth shut.

"Therefore, I beseech blessed Mary ever-Virgin—"

*Floating in the void.*

"Michael the Archangel—"

. *Cheeks puffed out, lips pressed shut.*

"—and you, brethren—"

*Spindly arms and legs blowing in the cosmic breeze.*

"—to pray to the Lord our God for me."

The priest was swaying, clockwise against the spin of the asteroid below. Marcus latched onto the movement, dredging himself from the vision, focusing on the shining crown atop the man's head.

"May Almighty God have mercy on us, forgive us our sins, and bring us to everlasting life."

The priest stilled. Silence fell on the chapel. Even the station's ever-present hum was gone.

Marcus held his breath, but the priest didn't budge, waiting for him to close the confession. He held on a little longer before blurting out, "Amen." It felt like razor blades on his tongue.

"Amen," the priest repeated. "Lord have mercy."

One of the censers sighed up ahead. The incense within it flared, crackled, discharging an errant thread of smoke that curled up toward the ceiling, lingering there, resisting the pull of the air exchangers. For a moment, the scent shifted to sickly sweet.

"Let us pray," the priest called, pulling Marcus back to the altar.

The man's arms were upraised, his eyes squeezed shut, his lips moving in quiet prayer. Discordant whispers buzzed about the empty pews. The censer continued its unruly hiss, joined by the uneven sputter of candles all around him, as though their electric flames were caught in the same breeze.

"Amen!"

The priest struck both palms against the altar, summoning silence back into the room.

Once again, Marcus's body reacted in kind, hands throbbing. He realized then he was still clutching his helmet. It vibrated in his hands. The sweat along his neck seal chilled. Reluctantly, he set it down on the pew, unsure if he should sit next to it or remain standing. Before he could decide, the priest's voice boomed forth.

"He that dwelleth in the aid of the most High, shall abide under the protection of the God of Jacob."

Marcus didn't know the proper response, or even what psalm this was. He glanced about for a hymnal but found none.

The priest didn't wait.

"He shall say to the Lord: Thou art my protector, and my refuge, my God, in him will I trust."

Again, Marcus tried to focus on the words, but again he found himself unmoored. There was only the cadence, tugging at him like the shifting tide. The priest's rising voice bore him up on waves, promising refuge upon the shore. But when it fell away, he fell with it, spiraling into a bottomless abyss filled with chanting of another sort.

"—thou shalt not be afraid of the terror of the night—"

The priest grasped the altar as though sensing his dismay, and Marcus followed, clutching the pew in front of him. An anchor in the storm.

"—of the business that walketh about in the dark: of invasion, or of the noonday devil—"

Verses rose and fell, sometimes so loud that they seemed shouted directly into his ear. Sometimes so distant that he wondered if they had been said at all.

*For he hath given his angels charge over thee.*

*In their hands they shall bear thee up.*

*He shall cry to me, and I will hear him.*

*And I will show him my salvation.*

Pages turned, each slicing like a blade in the dark.

Uneven footsteps.

From the mist, the priest's eyes emerged. His lips moving, disjointed words breaking through.

"—the light of thy body is thy eye—"

"—if thy eye be evil, thy whole body shall be full of darkness—"

The missal shut with a thud.

"The Gospel of the Lord," the priest declared.

Marcus lurched back into himself. The fog persisted, altar and priest blurred together. He blinked, flushing with heat as tears slipped down his cheeks, then scrubbed them away with the rough heel of his glove. When he could finally see again, the priest was just standing there.

Staring at him.

Waiting for something.

Marcus shuffled, looking everywhere but back. Finally, the priest returned to the altar, spread out the corporal, then placed the paten and hosts atop it.

An anxious gurgle rolled through his guts.

The priest bowed low while wiping his hands on his stole,

compulsively as though using a sanitary wipe. "Take this, all of you," he called, "for this is my body, which will be given up for you." He lifted one of the hosts over his head, bowed again, crossed himself, then lowered it into his mouth.

Marcus gritted his teeth at the sound, deep and grinding, like Martian basalt chewed through a tunneling machine.

The priest turned, the second host trembling in his hand. "The Body of Christ," he said. His other hand was upraised, as if to steady—or strike. His collar was dark with sweat.

Marcus tried and failed to step out of the pew. He glanced down at his helmet, to check if Sentry Mode had kicked in again, but the HUD was off while detached.

Just nerves.

He tried again, this time stumbling into the aisle and up toward the altar. Ignoring the imagined vacuum beyond his mouth as he opened it, the surging nausea as the host touched his tongue, and the urge to regurgitate it once he swallowed. "Amen," he choked out.

The priest lowered his hands, crossing himself and Marcus. "It is done," he said. He looked exhausted, shoulders slumped and eyes robbed of their prior gleam. "Thank you for coming." With that, he shuffled toward the door.

Marcus watched him go, slow to gather up the bits of himself scattered by the ritual. He desperately wanted something to drink. "Wait," he finally called, grabbing his helmet and following after the priest. There was more to be done here. Protocol. "I have questions."

The priest was already hiking up his vestments, preparing for another round at the door.

"Father, wait," Marcus insisted. A report was required. And for any report, he needed to confirm identity. "I need your name."

The priest stopped, let go of his chasuble, and once more

rubbed at the fading cross on its front. Without looking back at Marcus, he replied, "James." Between his lilting accent and fatigue, it almost sounded like a question.

"Father James..." Marcus said. What was the first question to ask? The most important thing? "What did you mean when you said, 'they go outside to pray'?"

The abomination's answer rang in his head before the priest's.

*Administrator Marshall is currently off-site.*

Doing what?

Father James continued to stare at the door. Marcus understood this as an invitation to leave but stayed put.

"Very well," Father James said. "Meet me in the sacristy in a few minutes. I need to clean up."

Marcus nodded and watched the man go. He would be glad for the reprieve.

The priest limped back up the aisle, his bad leg dragging more heavily than before. He doused the censers along the way, lingering beside each of them as they hissed out a final, pungent exhale, before closing with a whispered prayer.

For the first time, Marcus noticed gaps along the wall where some of the chapel's candles had expended their batteries. In other nooks, their artificial guttering had fallen out of sync, slowing toward darkness. If they had been manufactured on Earth, there would be no replacements forthcoming.

Father James paused at the altar, spoke a final prayer, then disappeared into the curtained-off submodule that served as both sacristy and quarters. The moment the curtains stilled, Marcus replaced his helmet, latched it, and dropped the visor. The unscented air from his recyclers was a mercy. He activated his hydration tube and sucked back half the suit's supply. It slaked his thirst but barely touched the lingering burn on his tongue and the back of his throat. Fortunately, there were menus and meters to get lost in.

He tapped compulsively around his HUD, checking on suit statuses and bio-monitors that were more aware of his body than he was. Ducking in and out of files he would eventually finish, making nominal edits—a punctuation change here, a second of audio clipped off there.

Only after a session of extended fiddling did he realize he hadn't checked his chronometer beforehand. It read 06:11. Probably enough.

Lifting his visor back up with a sigh, he followed the priest's footsteps to the sacristy. There was no chime or, God forbid, a bell. Just a dark red curtain, strung across the wall like a bloody bandage. He knocked on the adjacent bulkhead.

"Come," the priest called.

Marcus brushed the fabric aside and entered. The submodule was dark save for a pool of lamplight illuminating a steel desk near the front. Father James was already seated, hands clasped in front of him. A second chair was pushed out and waiting.

Beyond the priest, the room faded into shadow. It was similar to Marcus's own hab pod, but slightly larger and with additional storage, double-wide lockers on one side and a wall cabinet on the other. Vague silhouettes peeked from the cubbies, whatever trappings the priest had brought with him from Earth. The only visible ornamentation was a crucifix hanging above the headboard of the cot, identical to the one in the corridor.

"Sit," Father James said, his tone slightly more relaxed than last time.

The man's features were hidden beyond the ring of light. All Marcus could make out was a squared-off jaw demarcated by lips stained the same red as the curtain. And he could smell it now: open wine beneath the cloying residue of frankincense.

"I'd rather stand," Marcus said. "The suit—"

"The chair will hold you. Sit and speak freely."

Marcus balked. He wasn't here for confession. Not with a drunken priest.

The man's eyes emerged from the shadows, neither foggy nor weak. "Sit."

The command hit Marcus like a suit override. He complied, lowering himself onto the steel chair. It creaked under his weight, front legs splaying slightly, but held. Even so, he sat near the front, mag boots pressed hard into the floor in case he needed a quick exit.

"I... I need to record this conversation," Marcus said, hand moving to his terminal. "Do you consent?"

The priest's eyes flashed. "I do not."

Marcus hesitated. The question was a formality, not something that could be refused. An imperial assessor's jurisdiction was total.

"Why are you here?" Father James asked.

Marcus's hand swayed above the record button. "To review station operations," he said.

The priest said nothing.

Marcus adjusted his posture, stilling when the chair let loose another creak. Clearing his throat, he recapped his mandate, for posterity. "Shipping disruptions from the asteroid belt have reached critical levels. The last scheduled shipment from Psyche Station never arrived. I was sent to investigate."

Father James leaned forward, his chiseled profile cutting through the darkness. "Why are you *here*?"

*Safe harbor*.

An itch rose at the back of Marcus's throat. He tried to swallow it down, but it wouldn't budge. He lowered his hand, now clammy within its glove. The other one too. His whole body slicked with sweat against his compression layer.

"What have you seen?" the priest pressed.

Marcus darted his eyes around, looking for a heads up display that wasn't there. Without the suit computer to guide him, there were only his own disjointed thoughts and memories, both of which he had been avoiding.

What had he seen?

Anomalies, yes. Infractions. But also other... phenomena. Illogical. Unexplainable. Sights and sounds that hewed too close to the ranting reports of Ceres Station's administrator. Reports that any sane person would dismiss out of hand. Testing him. His mind. His soul.

"I... I'm not sure."

The dreams, too. Calling him to the void. Calling him to 16 Psyche.

He had to go there. To open the door—

No.

He had to go there. To find the administrator. To see for himself what she was up to. Any other compulsion was a trick of the mind, his subconscious tormenting him for his procrastination.

"It's falling apart," he said. "The station. As though it's been abandoned." Except for the cluster of gangly humanoids waiting in the hub. He shivered in his armor, undone by his own fears spoken aloud. "But that doesn't make sense. There's nothing out there."

"Space is not empty," Father James intoned. "It is full. Of evil."

"What?"

Marcus's temples were throbbing. His helmet felt too tight, as though fitted for someone else. He glanced down at his wrist terminal, but the microdisplay only showed the time. No heart rate, no blood pressure—no data. He counted his breaths instead, forcing them into rhythm.

"I have seen it before," the priest continued. "On the Moon."

"The Moon?"

Father James unclasped his hands and brushed his lips, then inspected the pink stain left on his fingertips. He rubbed them together, but the color lingered, glowing beneath the lamplight. "A long time ago. It's in our nature to seek, to stare up at the stars and wonder. But it is possible to look too far."

Marcus thought back to his colonial history. There had been an incident on the Moon years before Mars was fully colonized. A once in an era solar storm, followed by a temporary evacuation. But it was just a blip in humanity's persistent flight from war-torn Earth.

"What does that have to do with Psyche Station?" he asked.

Father James leaned forward, ensnaring Marcus with his gaze. His chest was heaving, his breath loud. "Space is the event horizon between Creation and uncreation. The void in which foul things linger. Uninvited. Rejected. Jealous of those chosen by the Lord."

"Cast out..." Marcus muttered, though he wasn't sure why.

"Yes," Father James hissed.

Marcus shook his head, tore his eyes away, focusing instead on his hands. He pressed them against his thigh plates, his boots hard into the floor, bracing against the drag of the station as it spun endlessly in space.

In for four breaths, hold, out for four.

No. This was nonsense. The ranting of a man too long on his own, farther from home even than Marcus. Long-term space travel didn't just affect the body, but the mind as well. It was well documented. He gritted his teeth and ran the list: depression, anxiety, paranoia—

Father James was whispering something.

—heightened suggestibility.

When Marcus looked up again, the man's eyes were glazed over. He took the opportunity to reexamine the module: windowless, cramped, as dark as the void and just as isolating. No terminal or other anchor to the world outside. A perfect breeding ground for psychosis, made worse by drink.

"How long have you been alone here?" Marcus asked.

Father James sank back into his seat, brow furrowing. The intensity drained from his face, leaving the deep lines around his eyes and mouth exposed. "I've lost track."

Marcus straightened as the other man shrank. His headache faded into the background. "When is the last time you spoke to Administrator Marshall?"

Father James winced as though struck.

"Father?"

"I'm not sure. She's been gone longer than the rest."

"Gone where?"

Father James pointed at the floor with a trembling finger. "Down there."

"The mining facility," Marcus said, slowly.

Father James didn't reply.

Marcus pushed past the sudden twinge in his stomach. "What are they doing there?" Clearly not their jobs, or Mars would be flush with resources.

"Digging at things that should be left alone."

The lamplight fizzed, blooming more brightly for a split second. Marcus blinked, but an afterimage remained, superimposed over the priest's chest. A rectangle in place of a cross. A mountain that was also a door. He blinked again, and it was gone.

"They can't all be there," he said.

"I don't know."

"It's been three years. You must know something."

Father James's eyes widened. "Three years. Three years... Has it really been that long?"

"Since the first shortfalls, yes."

The priest glanced sideways, in the direction of the chapel doors. "The corridors have seemed quieter for a while."

"So, you do leave the chapel."

"Yes," Father James said.

Marcus thought back to the thumping outside his pod—harried footsteps.

"To the mess hall," the priest added, "for supplies." He rubbed unconsciously at his mouth.

"What happened? How did it get this bad?"

Father James looked down, eyes darting as he searched his addled memories. "Mass was always poorly attended. On the best days, I only ever saw half the crew. But never Administrator Mar—" He grimaced, as though her name tasted rotten on his tongue. "Never the administrator." He grasped his stole and wrung it in his hands. "I remember one day, no one showed up. It happened on occasion. There were always emergencies. But this time there was no alarm, no comms. I walked the whole station and found it empty. Nothing on the docking bay logs. I assumed something had happened at the mine and returned to my quarters."

"Did you ask Central Receiving?" Marcus asked.

Father James wrinkled his nose. "Her pet. No. I don't talk to it."

Marcus nodded approvingly, but wondered at the priest's aversion to the station administrator. He made a mental note to ask later. "Go on."

"It was never the same after that. Half became half a dozen, then a few, then none. And not just Mass. I ate alone, exercised alone. The mail drops stopped. Eventually, I stopped. Without a flock, I was lost."

"Did you try to send a message out?" Marcus asked. No distress signals had been mentioned in his briefing, no signals at all. Just a dwindling ledger.

"I tried, but I was locked out. Hacking a door panel is one thing. Hacking relay access is entirely another."

"Tell me about that."

"The doors?"

"Yes."

Father James took a long, stabilizing breath.

"It was quiet for a long time. Then one night, I heard yelling. When I went outside, I saw a group of them, still wearing their spacesuits. Dragging another who wasn't. He was... He was screaming. In a voice not his own. Not any one man's voice... Many voices."

The module shifted beneath Marcus's feet. The station's pulse vibrated through his legs into his chest, replacing his own heartbeat. He pressed his lips together, but the question forced its way out.

"What was he saying?"

Father James let go his stole and crossed himself. "*Sancte Míchael Archángele, defénde nos in proélio...*" Then crossed himself a second time. "Old words," he said. "Terrible words."

*A command that will open the way.*

"Assessor?"

Father James was staring at him. Marcus's breath caught in his throat.

"You look a little green. Would you like some water?"

Marcus waved the priest's concerns away, even as he found himself suddenly lightheaded. Bands of color danced in the corners of the room. "Continue."

Father James lingered a moment, then tugged at his chasuble and leaned back in his chair. "I tried to help, but they wouldn't let me. Each time I got close, one of them would push me away. It wasn't until the screaming man nearly broke free that I saw who it was: Technician Rowley. He had been a regular many years past, then disappeared with the rest. I barely recognized him. He was... changed. Thinner, taller. Eyes as black as the void. Gasping as though he had forgotten how to breathe. And the smell..."

"The smell?"

"Like the sea, after it died."

Marcus thought back to his rendezvous with the station shuttle, the phantom odor that crept in alongside the pilot. He had never seen or smelled something as inconceivable as a sea, never would, but he knew it in that moment. Of the pilot himself, he had seen very little: dark eyes behind a dark visor.

"I retreated. Back here," Father James said, taking up his stole again. His jaw flexed in the shadow. "The power in Section C shut off that night."

"A malfunction?"

"A warning. By the grace of God, I still had life support and partial grid access. Enough to look through my camera whenever I heard them outside." He gestured at the lamp. "And enough to read by."

This was more than dereliction of duty. If the priest's tale was accurate, it was mutiny.

If.

"This is madness," Marcus muttered.

"Yes, it was. I struggled. I prayed. And then, one day, I began keeping the rites—Mass, the Hours. It helped, so I kept doing it, and found a measure of peace. Of purpose."

Silence settled on the room.

Marcus had sought both spiritual and factual support and found neither. The man's testimony was too fractured, distorted by his extended isolation. He would have to cross-reference everything against his download later. Check station logs and CCTV archives. Establish a timeline. Away from the chapel and the stink of incense and sacramental wine.

But first, he would have to speak with the returned crew. He had no choice.

"I think that will be enough," he said, and began to stand.

"You're wondering if I'm a drunk."

Marcus stopped, unsure how to respond.

"I do not drink to escape," Father James said. "I drink to bind myself to Christ, who is so very far away."

Marcus lifted himself from the chair. "I am here to assess, not to judge."

"I wish I could do the same..."

Marcus racked his brain for something consoling. "I will likely be recommending a crew rotation. I'll make sure you're on the first exchange."

"No."

Marcus frowned. "No?"

"I fled danger once before." Father James rubbed at his leg, gaze drawn to another place and time. "God put me here for a reason. I will stay to see it through."

"But it's not just Section C. The whole station is on the brink."

And Mars with it.

The priest pushed himself out of his chair, bracing against the desk. "I'll see you out." With that, he led the way from the sacristy.

Marcus stumbled after him, unable to produce a logical argument. It didn't matter; he would put in the transfer request anyway.

When they reached the entrance, Father James repeated his

control pad ritual, peering through his camera until satisfied it was safe to proceed, then cranking the doors open.

"Thank you again for coming," he said, stepping close to Marcus. His mouth moved some more but no additional words came. His head shook fractionally. Finally, he made the sign of the cross and intoned, "*Dominus vobiscum.*"

Marcus stepped from the chapel into the dark.

# 10
# PROTOCOL

The stomachache hit immediately.

Marcus took a few sips from his hydration tube, but the solitary Communion wafer weighed heavy in his guts, slowing his steps as he progressed through the rest of Section C. Only the need for careful navigation served to distract him. Panning his meager helmet light around. Dodging fallen ceiling panels and ruts in the floor. The physical damage worsened the farther he went.

Up ahead, an amber glow marked the second sanitation bay, the last module in the section. Marcus shifted his attention to the floor as he approached. The grime was thick, marked by indistinct shapes and smears. He didn't linger or look too hard this time. The psych eval he had given the priest weighed as much on his mind as the wafer in his stomach, along with the possibility he was just as susceptible.

Hurrying on, he proceeded to Spoke D, nearly colliding with the inner bulkhead several times along the way. The decommissioned transit lift appeared without warning. No barricades or placards, just an empty shaft and an emergency ladder. The priest's gang of crewmen must have come down when it still worked, and blocked the entrance after.

Marcus glanced back the way he'd come, his helmet light fading in the distance. If they were taking one of their own to Medical, Spoke B would have made more sense. They clearly weren't headed for the chapel, and unlikely any of the rec bays.

Which left only the storage modules.

He held his breath, listening for knocks, the faint jingle of chains. The darkness swallowed all sound other than the station's subsonic thrum.

Bracing himself, he activated multispectral mode.

Zigzag distortions crackled across his visor as infrared, thermal, and positional data were fused together. The corridor resolved from nothing into a radiant sepia wireframe, its geometry laid bare. A moment later it filled in, each panel shading into solid form. Shifting heat signatures billowed like fog across the ceiling and floor. The corridor was otherwise empty, curving up and away into oblivion.

This time, Marcus lingered. Just to be sure.

Faint constellations twinkled within dying junction boxes. Conduits pulsed in rhythm to the station's heartbeat. But no man or beast trailed after him. Only a dim pang of guilt at leaving the priest behind.

He reset his visor and continued to Section D. Past the spoke, the ceiling lights flickered on again, as though nothing were wrong. The dilapidation returned to its prior, less alarming state. Each pod door was still marked with red.

D-1, D-2... He stepped gingerly, though the report of his mag boots was hard to suppress.

When he reached D-8, he moved immediately to the control pad and opened his visor just long enough to activate the scanner. The pad flashed green and the door rumbled open. Everything was as he had left it. His suitcase was ready to go.

He hung there long enough for the twinge in his gut to reappear, then opened his HUD menu to Suit Storage. All of Psyche Station's log data was right there, plus the CCTV feeds he had channeled, and his own sparse dictation. Everything except the priest's verbal testimony, which he had failed to record.

Not enough.

He brought up the CCTV snapshot and dragged the playhead to the end, to the clustered crewmen. The frame juddered in place, threatening to break free. He quickly copied the camera ID, closed the window, and ran a search on it. The station schematic popped up, centered on a camera midway down the hub, at the "top," as he had suspected. Spoke A, the upside down one, would be closest. He also wouldn't have to circumnavigate from floor to ceiling once he arrived.

His stomach twinged again.

Marcus dismissed his HUD windows and palmed the door shut. The control pad blinked back to red. He turned into the corridor and marched past the final two hab pods to his destination.

The spoke was empty when he got there. He pressed the call button and flinched as a mechanical squeal echoed down the shaft. Leaning in, he watched the lift lumber downward, grinding into its rails as it took on weight. Weight he would soon lose once he was back in the hub. He was glad for it this time; his bones ached.

Halfway down, the whole spoke began to rattle, as though ready to shear off. He stepped back and grabbed a handhold, waiting nervously until it settled to the deck with a thud and a slow eruption of dust.

The lift's condition was no better than the others. He paused before boarding, just in case his suit had any different ideas. But no new alerts popped up on his HUD. No algorithms took control of his limbs. He stepped inside, steadied himself for the gravity shift, and pressed Up.

The first few meters tugged at his body in all the wrong ways, but the discomfort faded as he neared zero-g. His arms floated up and out. His legs as well, which he reluctantly magnetized back into place with a tap at his wrist. It was like leaving his body behind—like his dreams. He allowed his eyes to drift shut. The noise faded. The vibration settled. There was only the sensation of floating.

*Across viridian canyons. Toward the iron mountain.*

A muted clunk ran through the lift as it docked.

Too soon.

Marcus opened his eyes, finding himself at the junction. Central Receiving loomed above him along with the haphazard route he had taken from the dock. Though bolted in place and absent gravity, the server racks looked ready to crash downward —or upward—releasing the abomination from its silicon prison.

He reoriented straight ahead. Past the junction was a parallel walkway leading to the alcoves where the crew was lurking. A curtain of chain links and loose cable hung at the entrance, rippling in the breeze of a nearby supply fan. Beyond it was the tangled cargo netting that spanned the cylinder. It was impossible to see inside.

With one hand fastened to the guardrail, he moved up, mag boots snapping hard onto the deck. Only by sheer force of will did he avoid looking up, which was also down.

The curtain greeted him with a discordant singsong, like an out-of-tune windchime. He ducked low, contorting his way through. Wandering hooks snatched at his suit, curling around his waist and into empty gear latches. Each time he swatted them away, the chiming grew more insistent. By the time he cleared it, almost tumbling out the other side, disorientation had fully set in. A handful of LED banks shimmered from deeper inside, but they cast more shadow than light.

Marcus turned on his mini-map and helmet light. No multi-spectral mode this time, in case it revealed more than he wanted to see. He pressed on, carefully detaching himself from the deck plates where necessary. Up and over walls, by handhold where available, and short glides through dead space when not. Direction became meaningless, even as he checked his progress on the HUD. As before, there was no sound of work, no tools or idle chatter to follow. It was only when the beam from his helmet reflected back at him that he realized he had found them.

The crew.

They just hung there, as they had in the feed: five conjoined silhouettes, unmoving and unmoved by his presence, save for a languorous swaying back and forth. Long limbs protruding from the dark, faces shaded over.

Behind them, a chiseled wall of alien ore loomed like a reredos, flaring wherever Marcus panned his helmet light. Rusted veins of red and gold throbbed beneath the surface, geometric patterns shimmering across every cut.

An error message flashed on his HUD as his visor tried and failed to compensate.

"I..." he started, but panic stopped him there. Bands of pink and purple strobed across his vision whichever way he moved. He wanted to kill the light but not to be left with *them* in the darkness.

Squinting through watery eyes, he toggled his visor to straight thermal.

The glare vanished.

The crew delineated, colored in, but different from what he remembered in OSSM low-light training. Their signatures were cooler, pale blues and greens mirroring the reredos behind them, as if carved from the same stone. In place of eyes were dark hollows. No warmth anywhere.

Suddenly aware that he was floating their way, Marcus scrambled for purchase. His limbs shot out at speed, driven by the combat suit's stress response. One hand found the edge of a workbench and gripped hard, sending a metallic squeal through the labyrinth. The other hooked onto a wad of netting. He pulled himself back, narrowly avoiding a line of saw blades and bits that hung at the periphery like razor wire. The floor was nowhere to be found.

And still they were silent.

His compression layer tightened over his chest. Alternating pulses beat through his shoulders and arms. The suit wanted to fight.

"Be calm," he whispered, to himself and the suit.

They were just people, as people were this far out in space. Whatever the priest had warned. Whatever he had seen, or thought he had seen, with his own eyes.

Just people.

"Be calm," he repeated, breathing deeply past the urging of his suit.

Servos whirred down. Joints slackened.

The cold lines of their faces remained still, as though sleeping. They might be. After a long day of praying outside—

No.

Working. Off-site.

But if that were the case, his fumbling should have woken them. His eyes burned, but he waited to blink so as not to miss a movement.

Still nothing.

A tendril of agitation crept up his spine, preferable to terror. He let it grow, steeling himself with righteous indignation.

Protocol.

He finally blinked, then cleared the fear from his throat and tapped on his helmet speaker. "Who is the ranking technician here?"

It still came out weaker than intended.

One of them moved—or the slab of ore behind them, he wasn't sure. Whichever way he angled himself, worker and ore blended together.

"I am Imperial Assessor Marcus O., on priority dispatch from Mars. I need to speak to someone about the state of this station."

The same crewman shifted again, unfurling from the mass like an extended tentacle. Chromatic aberrations buzzed around the lanky green silhouette as it neared.

Marcus gripped the bench tighter, but held his ground, precarious as it was. "I have documented an unacceptable catalog of faults."

Closer.

He sped up. "Repairs are to be effected immediately."

The crewman's face stopped inches from his visor, but he could see no more detail than before. No more humanity. Just barren peaks and valleys, shifting beneath his optics.

"I demand participation."

A chasm split open in one of the valleys, black and bottomless. From it came an inhuman croak. "He demands..."

Marcus's blood turned to ice.

More sounds came from the others, then: gasping chortles, like metal scraping against stone.

The suit tensed again. Bio-monitors swelled on his HUD.

Marcus edged backward, only to find himself surrounded on all sides by partition walls. He braced his legs on opposing planes.

Protocol.

"Where is Administrator Marshall?" he asked, barely managing to restrain the tremor in his throat.

The chasm sealed shut. The crewman floated back into his cluster.

"I need to see her," Marcus insisted.

A hint of yellow sparked between them—behind them—but nothing more.

The pulsing that had coaxed his arms now moved to his legs.

It was time to go.

"Fine," he muttered. "I'll find someone else."

He waited several more ragged breaths before pushing off.

The labyrinth was nearly invisible under thermal, scant color protruding through the lattice of its artificial walls. Nothing was turned on. The machines were as cold as the crew. He waited until he was facing away from the pale figures to reactivate his helmet light, holding fast to irritation and contempt. Anything that suppressed the dread of their dark eyes drilling into his back. After a moment's scramble, he found the exit and rushed back the way he had come.

By the time he emerged from the still-churning portal, he was out of breath. He took a moment to rest and weigh his options, and to scold himself for his poor performance. He should have left his lights on. Noted each crewmember's name tag for his report. Persisted. Instead of getting caught up...

In their eyes.

And the way they moved—

07:30.

Marcus blinked as his chronometer turned over. Still an age until his scheduled departure. He should try again. Central Receiving squatted directly below him, the shining call bell inviting him to ring for assistance.

Not that. Never that.

But the pilot might be available. He could confirm the shuttle's timetable. And also corroborate some of the priest's testimony.

He marched back to the junction, set his mag boots to max, then turned and followed the walkway as it bent down and around the inside of the hub toward the floor proper. Landing was a relief, the disorientation somehow less. He gave the receiving desk a wide berth as he proceeded down the cargo line to the dock, trying not to think of the slumbering crewmen or their ill-gotten treasure.

The lower half of the hub was unoccupied, as before. Decontamination came up fast, its large bay doors open. At its terminus, the inner pressure door stood sealed, its status light a steady green. Beyond it lay the cargo airlock.

Marcus stepped to the control pedestal and checked the indicator once more before activating it. The door cycled open with a grudging groan, admitting him into the chamber beyond.

Two small portholes were set into the walls on either side of the outer pressure door. He stepped just inside and paused.

Nothing stirred. No motor whine or gears engaging to lock him in.

After one last look back at the hub—and Receiving—he walked to the left-hand window and pressed his visor to the rim.

The docking clamps were empty.

No shuttle.

No pilot.

No way home.

Every nerve in his body flared. He pressed harder, seeking a telltale twinkle amidst the stars. There was only 16 Psyche. Spinning in the void.

All-consuming.

The longer he looked, the more he could feel the station's rotation, even here at its center. He braced against the wall, centering on the asteroid's north pole. Despite the distance, the surface was clearly visible. Thrombotic veins, deep canyons, flashes of light refracting to the limits of the visible spectrum. Spiraling down and around, toward the equator and the mining site beyond. To the hidden horizon. The iron mountain.

His eyelids grew heavy.

The glass melted away. The porthole widened. He lifted from the deck and floated through, separated from the void only by the thinness of his visor. Carried on a winding current of solar wind.

Down and around.

Something hissed on his comms. No, it was coming from outside. Muffled chanting, beating a rhythm against his helmet. He could almost make it out, mouthing the words. So close. He only needed to release the latch on his collar—

"What are you doing?"

Gaping eyes stared at him from the window. He spun about, still stuck to the wall.

In the airlock.

His chest was pounding.

Someone was there—*something*. Hovering above him like an ascendant saint. Garbed in ratty gray coveralls. Barefoot. Long toenails dragging along the floor. As tall as Marcus was in his suit but a fraction as thick.

A once-man.

Marcus blinked, shook his head, but it didn't disappear. He forced his gaze upward, feeling ever shorter. Ever heavier. A servant to gravity.

The creature leered back at him, haloed by the flickering lights above its head. Pallid, mostly green, with dark red spots mottling its bare scalp—all the same colors the others had appeared under thermal imaging. What he could see of its oblong face was ringed with burns, approximating the outline of a helmet visor. And the eyes... pupil and iris joined into a single black orb, the scant white around them ruptured pink.

Had it spoken? Could such a thing speak?

He waited, stuck like a fly in a spider's web.

The creature shifted fractionally, its attention moving to the outer pressure door.

Marcus glanced sideways without moving any part of his body, following the line of his helmet to his arm, to his gloved hand. It was poised over the emergency release latch, fingers tense and twitching. The override switches had already been thrown. He watched in horror, willing them to stop moving, to release. Not to pull.

Scrutinized, the digits fell back one by one. The hand stilled. Marcus cinched it to his side and stared again at the person before him.

Just a person.

Not just a person.

In this moment, both were true. Marcus had seen similar on other stations, among those who had spent too long in the void, though not quite like this.

Nothing like this.

He compartmentalized—rapidly. Ran lists. Projected extreme physiological outcomes. Cutting off every part of him that wanted to flee, until the heart rate monitor that he only now realized had been screaming at him began to slow.

He breathed, waited.

Time slipped past, but the creature said nothing more.

He tried to remember why he had come here.

Protocol.

"The shuttle," Marcus stammered. "Where is my shuttle?"

The once-man floated backward, as though self-propelled. It was halfway through Decon before Marcus could make his legs work, slowly pursuing.

"Wait!"

It continued past the bay, lifting higher until only its flaccid feet were visible, and the fleshy membrane connecting its toes. Then those too disappeared, into a cloudscape of black mesh and the celestial labyrinth beyond.

The walls closed in.

Everything skewed sideways.

Whichever way Marcus looked, his HUD bled out all over the floor.

Whichever direction he moved, he was pushed in the opposite.

The floor...

There was a light. Steady.

And another farther on, pulsing in sequence. Then another beyond that.

He followed them, one heavy footstep after the other. Until his digital readouts stabilized and he no longer felt like his soul would spin free of his body.

Looking up, he found Central Receiving. The call bell waited for him.

He pressed it.

The abomination materialized almost instantly, as though it had been on standby the whole time. Seated, as before, within an aerosol haze. Featureless. Faceless.

Only then did he realize what he had done.

Too late.

"Welcome, Assessor," it said. "Please connect to the wireless network to proceed."

There was no intrusion warning this time, just a pulsing icon on his HUD indicating a peer-to-peer connection request.

Marcus watched himself tap OK.

His suit powered down with a pained whir. Compression,

climate control, joint assist—all systems dropped at once. The air grew chill and thin. His legs loosened from the deck.

Just as he felt himself about to lose balance again, everything sizzled back online. He jerked straight, snapped in. New processes erupted all over his visor and were immediately killed. Menus opened and closed. Station logs, personnel records, personal records. Every file stacked and interrogated at machine speed until they collapsed into a single blinking cursor.

The suit blipped three times.

The HUD reset, as though nothing had happened. But something had. His compression layer felt... wrong. Cycling in a new pattern. An itch crept along his abdomen and down his thighs, as though the suit were relearning the shape of him.

"Connection established," the blank declared. It almost sounded happy.

Slowly, the thing reconfigured. Its head fractured into polygons, each one subdividing again and again until cheek bones emerged; then a nose, long and straight; full lips; eyes the color of emeralds. A cascade of auburn hair followed, lagging behind the face, glitching at the edges.

It was Administrator Marshall, as she had been when the station launched.

"How may I assist you?" she asked.

*It.* It asked—the abomination.

Marcus shuddered, uncertain if this was better or worse.

Protocol.

A long moment passed as his voice crept from its hiding place. "I need to speak to—"

The abomination blinked, freezing Marcus mid-sentence.

A hologram shouldn't blink.

An array of micro-expressions rippled across its face, snapping into higher resolution wherever his gaze lingered. He hadn't noticed at first. It even seemed to be breathing, the simulated gray uniform rising and falling all the way to its six-fingered hands.

Acid rose in his throat but he swallowed it back.

"I need to speak to Administrator Marshall," he continued.

It blinked again. "Administrator Marshall is currently off-site."

As expected.

Marcus hesitated, prolonging the inevitable a few seconds longer.

"I need to go off-site."

The thing's lips curved in the guise of a smile. Its cheeks dimpled. Its eyes brightened, even as the lights around them dimmed and the station's pulse missed a beat. Behind it, the green status lights on the server racks swelled to the point of bursting.

Just as quickly, its expression neutralized. "No transit is currently available."

The budding panic from the empty dock returned. "Where is my shuttle?" he asked.

"Off-site."

Marcus clenched his fists, ready to pummel—

"Transit has been arranged."

That was new.

"A shipping drone has been recalled and will be available for boarding in approximately two hours." The blank interlaced its many fingers, satisfied with itself.

"A drone..."

"Recalled and available for boarding in two hours and twelve minutes."

"But a drone can't carry passengers."

"You will be accommodated."

Marcus tried to detect deception, but every answer the creature gave had the same cadence. The same absolute certainty. "Are you sure?"

"Your suit will provide the requisite life support."

"My suit... And if there's an emergency?"

"Your suit will provide the requisite life support," it repeated.

"What about my shuttle?"

"Off-site."

"I mean"—he gritted his teeth, trying to hold onto whatever calm he had left—"will it be back by 1800 hours?"

"Your shuttle is due at 1800 hours."

"Is that a yes?"

It smiled again, wider than last time. Synthesized textures collided where the corners of its mouth encroached upon its eyes. "Yes."

He hesitated, flinching as it blinked again. And again. As though daring him to shut it off, assuming his prior command had even worked. Too risky in any case. Whatever orders it had sent to the station's other machines might be disrupted. When he filed his assessment, he would order a full mainframe scrub along with the crew rotation.

The blank's smile disappeared, as though it had read his thoughts.

Marcus backed away from the desk. "Okay," he said. "I'll be in my quarters."

It didn't reply. It just sat there, pretending at life as he removed himself from Central Receiving and retreated from the hub as fast as humanly possible.

# 11
## 16 PSYCHE

Marcus stood in the corner of his pod and waited.

He considered returning to Operations, to update his snapshots and check on the live feed. Or refilling his suit reservoir in the galley. Or visiting Medical, to see if he could find any record of Technician Rowley's injuries. Or reconvening with Father James, to confess the sin of consorting with an artificial lifeform—of letting it into his suit.

He did none of those things.

For two hours and twelve minutes he fretted, procrastinated. Until his comms pinged and her voice whispered into his ear, "Transit has arrived."

His legs carried him from the room.

His hands activated the lift.

He watched from inside the cavern of his helmet as his body proceeded through the junction, past Central Receiving—empty once more—to the dock.

It was happening.

He was going off-site.

Both the inner and outer airlock doors were open and waiting for him—a severe breach of safety protocols. Infractions floated through his mind but dissolved just as quickly. He was too focused on the narrow slit on the other side, cut through a blackened and chipped hull. This was the drone's accommodation. Not a docking compartment but a maintenance shaft behind an open pressure door. Close-set, maybe a meter wide, slatted walls and thick veins of bundled cable extending into darkness.

He drifted through the airlock to the precipice. There were no guide lights or handholds. He thumbed on his helmet light, driving it deep into the ship's gullet. Arcane machinery glinted behind the mesh, turning to unknown purpose. Far off in the distance was another door, sealed flush with the bulkhead. Like the shaft itself, it was devoid of human interface.

But it would open. For him.

Disengaging his mag boots, he tipped forward—down, into it—pulling himself along the cables. They throbbed beneath his grip, faster than the station's pulse, skipping a beat each time his armor scraped the walls. His legs trailed behind him as he descended, kicking reflexively against nothing.

As he cleared the entrance, the drone's outer door sealed shut with a thud. His helmet light scattered. Direction disappeared, as it had in the labyrinth. Only this was much tighter. Darker.

The second door wheezed open, drawing in what little atmosphere had followed him. Marcus craned his head up to look. On the other side shone a single pinprick of light. He clawed toward it, the clang of his suit and heaving breath distorting into a ragged chorus. By the time he got there, his forehead was slick with sweat, servo assist in full gear.

He poked his head through the opening into a cramped cockpit. Or a cell. Whatever the room was, it was tiny. There was no window or recliner. Just a wall harness and a supplemental oxygen line opposite a terminal. The screen glared uselessly beneath his helmet light. He shut it off and was presented with a flashing data jack icon. It was waiting for him.

His fingers tightened on the doorframe.

He watched the screen flash on and off.

Then he was in the harness, straps cinching across his chest. The last buckle clipped shut. The data jack slid from his wrist and locked in.

A message popped onto his HUD.

READY FOR LAUNCH. EXECUTE?

His finger hovered for a long moment over his wrist terminal, then tapped OK.

The inner door slammed shut. A timer appeared in place of the message, counting down from sixty seconds. Maneuvering thrusters fired up, sending a vibration through every surface, every bone in his body.

He tried to look around but was jammed tight. There was nothing to do but stare at the screen and wait.

The timer hit.

Mooring clamps disengaged.

The drone kicked free with a shriek and immediately braked against the station's rotation—too hard.

The walls spun, weaving into a cocoon. Layer upon layer of steel turned to sticky thread. Smothering his legs, arms, then his visor. Filling his ears and mouth. Suffocating him before he could scream—

*Cheeks puffed out.*

*Lips pressed shut.*

*A hand in his. The same as his. Long fingers, sallow green skin.*

*Naked in the void.*

Marcus gasped awake, flailing against the dark. Belts crisscrossed his chest, a bar against his waist. Pinning him.

The command room.

The drone.

He had rung the bell.

It felt like a dream. A nightmare.

Hazy figures swam across his visor. He dredged himself back, focused, found the chronometer. Only a few minutes had passed since the drone launched.

A new meter hovered beside the time, displaying oxygen reserves. This one showed five hours, though the number fluctuated more and more the longer he watched. Four and a half. Four forty-nine. Five oh-six. Hitching with each uneven breath.

There was always the backup. The ship's supply line drifted just past his helmet, tip wagging and rimmed with green frost. Not that he was in a hurry to plug in, given the likely stench. Assuming it even worked.

The count dropped from five hours to four.

He should have thought of that. Run the numbers.

Condensation blossomed and died on his helmet. Another ten minutes shaved off.

He held his breath until it crawled back up, then inhaled slowly through his teeth.

"Be calm," he whispered.

Forcing himself to look away, he brought up the shipping drone's master menu.

AUTONOMOUS MINING CRAFT PS-D-8

D-8… like his pod.

Reserved just for him.

He swallowed back another surge of anxiety and tapped through to Passenger Interface. Several windows popped onto his HUD, displaying trajectory, ship status, and a forward camera feed. A wireframe render of the asteroid slid beneath them, overlaid with annotated curves and waypoints tracing the drone's transit to the mining facility on the south pole. The real 16 Psyche loomed off to the side. Tapping onto the feed, he cycled cameras until it appeared front and center.

Now that he was up close, it looked... familiar. A sketch solidified into bold strokes, like revisiting a place he had been as a child. Every crevice and pit. Every mineral deposit bursting to the surface. Streaks of color emerging wherever sunlight permitted.

Only as natural formations gave way to machine-made lines did the sense of familiarity falter. Canyons that had been static for millennia widened into great trenches, splitting and rejoining in a spiral maze algorithmically plotted to maximize extraction. He tried to follow them, but the logic was too complex, the geometries in the exposed strata too dizzying. The camera seemed to struggle as well, fragmenting into digital noise wherever the cuts ran too deep. Eventually he gave up, zooming out for a broader view, skimming rather than delving. The image cleared, but something nagged at him.

It was too clear.

He zoomed out some more. Aside from the visual artifacts, the surface was unobstructed. No debris cloud or other signs of active mining.

Carefully, he panned over to the ends of the maze where the crawlers should be, chewing away at the surface. Ducking and weaving whenever the camera got hung up. He found one on a solitary run, its bulbous body and huge robotic legs reduced by distance, but still large enough that he could plainly see it was stationary. Not damaged, just inactive. Like a lab rat that had given up after hitting too many dead ends.

He backed out and located another one on the opposite horizon, also inactive.

Crawlers were never supposed to stop. Except for emergency maintenance and when their bellies were full, just long enough for a hauler to mount them and relieve them of their payload. Crawler to hauler to processing to shipping drone—that was protocol. The mining site status reports had given the impression of a smooth operation.

Maybe because it wasn't operating at all.

Marcus minimized the live feed and brought up his log snapshots, shifting irritably as his right arm kept knocking against the harness. He couldn't even enjoy microgravity in the bowels of this cursed machine.

In separate windows, he loaded individual crawler statuses, site processing throughput, and inventory movement. Painstakingly sorting and cross-referencing until a pattern emerged from the glut of data. Three of the crawlers had ceased digging at the same time as shipments to Mars dropped off. Inspecting each of them, he could find no faults. They were simply full, stuck in standby mode waiting for unloads that never came.

The rest were all clumped together in a single quadrant farther on. Those had continued to dig, serviced by haulers until a few months ago when they stopped as well.

The camera feed shifted then, from jagged lines to straight.

He had arrived.

Marcus relocated the feed to the right half of his visor and stared, momentarily struck dumb. Like all architecture of the colonial enterprise, the mining facility was vast and brutalist. A regurgitated template of platforms, processing drums, and storage shafts, run through by massive conveyors and loomed over with robotic cranes. More machine hive than habitat. In this case, not a habitat at all. The only shelter proffered to humans was in the narrow service passages worming through its green-tinted superstructure, there to keep the site and its servitor machines running.

Everything looked intact, but as dead as the crawlers. And darkened by a shadow that surpassed that of the surrounding basin.

He zoomed out a little, to the staging areas that surrounded the facility. The hauler drones sat idle on their landing pads, piles of unprocessed ore pressing in around them. As he tapped out farther, the piles only grew, rising into a great curved wall that stretched above the lip of the basin. Towering over the facility like a tsunami frozen by the vacuum of space, threatening to pulverize it back to raw regolith.

Marcus gawked.

Backups happened, but not like this. There were failsafes, automated and manual. Redundancies. Protocols. They had all failed.

Before he could recover, another pile came into view, this one orderly, rectangular. Cargo modules. Dozens of them, unhitched and left behind by their shipping drones.

He scanned the skies above: empty. And his own ship wasn't slowing down.

*Administrator Marshall is currently off-site.*

Off-site where? There was no one here.

He raced through the logs to find last known drone locations. Long arrays of coordinates scrolled down the screen, meaningless except for the fact that they matched the location of the remaining crawlers.

They were all there, wherever *there* was.

He collapsed every window on his HUD save the feed, expanding it to the limit of his visor.

The ship's altitude was dropping. 16 Psyche writhed beneath him, no longer rendered passive by distance. The facility gave way to more trenches, deeper than the others.

Much deeper, much darker, stained red at the edges. Stretching outward rather than in, as though searching for something. Then converging back toward his present course. The surface sank, regraded by years—decades—of constant, focused excavation, before cutting away completely into a sheer cliff.

The horizon simply disappeared.

Marcus pressed back into his harness as vertigo hit. His stomach lurched. The feed blurred and spun sideways, but not from dizziness. The ship was turning. Decelerating. The vibration ran straight through him, shaking every buckle and strap so that they drummed against his armor. He fumbled at his wrist terminal until a rear-facing camera popped onto his HUD.

Beyond the precipice, something new had appeared: a singular structure at the far end of the void. At first, he could only see its peak. Not a point but a line, stretching straight across the gap where the body of the asteroid had once been. Then widening as it dropped, deeper and deeper into the abyss.

An iron mountain.

Torn free from the surrounding rock, its outer face machined smooth. Great seams ran across it like a door. Though opposite the sun, it glowed with a pale light of its own, gathered from the distant stars.

Outshining them.

Marcus's eyes burned but he couldn't blink. Tears beaded on his lashes as the structure plummeted downward, terminating at last at the bottom of the great pit from which it had been carved. The whole excavation must have been a kilometer deep and three wide.

Clustered at the base were the remaining crawlers. Tiny at this scale, their great legs folded inward, prostrated before the mountain—the door.

The angle shifted as the ship pitched toward them. Acrid

water flooded his eyes. He batted at his terminal until a blast of air scoured them dry, blinking at last.

More of the floor slid into view. Past the crawlers, parked in a concentric ring about the base of the door, were Psyche Station's shipping drones.

All of them.

He blinked again, fighting floaters at the edges of his vision. Only they weren't floaters. They were figures, far below. Long. Lanky. Just standing there in their spacesuits—hovering. Before the door.

He zoomed in.

Some of them had their visors open.

"No..."

Impossible.

"No, no, no."

He smashed at his terminal, but his fingers were rigid, uncooperative. He shut his eyes and kept trying. The feed finally disconnected with a click. Cracking his eyes open again, he kept tapping until the other windows were all gone. His dwindling oxygen meter flashed in the corner.

Hypoxia. Yes.

Or exhaustion. Too long in the void.

The afterimage of burned faces drifted across his vision.

No. He saw it.

He saw it.

An incoming comms icon popped up. No source.

"What?"

His suit auto acknowledged.

"No. Wait."

It didn't.

A burble of static spilled into his helmet, interspersed with stretches of hard noise that sent a shock down his jaw and into every one of his decaying teeth. He leaned forward, tried to grab at his helmet as if it would help, but the harness blocked him.

The signal shifted as the suit computer compensated, filtered, compressed. Until the background static harmonized into a chanted chorus and the noise approximated words.

Old words.

Terrible words.

Words he could almost understand, if only he would repeat them.

*A command that will open the way.*

Between *here* and *there.*

Somewhere beyond the door. Beyond Creation. Blacker even than the void.

His lips moved, feeling the shape of them. Summoning impossible sounds from his throat. Sounds that only a once-man could make—

The signal broke apart.

His jaw clamped shut. Pain flared. Blood filled his mouth.

His whole body was shaking, along with the ship. In place of digital noise came the transmitted clacking of landing gear deploying. Loud enough to detune his comms.

To snap him back, if only for a moment.

Here.

He needed to stay *here.*

"Override," he gasped.

Not the right word.

"Override. Override."

Not the right word!

What was the number?

"Compliance override code 22..."

His tongue was twice as thick as it should be.

"226432... 42."

A command cursor appeared on his HUD.

He swallowed, choked on his own blood, spat it back up onto his visor.

"Return. To station. Full burn!"

OVERRIDE ACCEPTED

His organs mashed together as the shipping drone changed course, accelerating out of the pit. The signal screamed, then faded back into static and noise. He clutched at his restraints, refusing to black out this time, staring at his HUD until the comms icon finally blinked off.

Though he couldn't see the surface anymore, he could feel it falling back. 16 Psyche's marginal gravity tugging at his soul one last time before disconnecting.

The drone twisted and turned, barreling around the asteroid and back to the station. Then quieted all at once as its thrusters disengaged. All that was left was an arrhythmic rattling in his chest, maybe his own weakened heart.

Marcus hung in silence. Terrified. Not only by what he had seen—or hadn't, couldn't have—but by the ship itself. And his own suit, which had betrayed him. He was trapped, within a machine, within a machine. A pittance of treacherous metal and composite separated him from the void.

He scanned the edges of his visor. Nothing crawled out.

What was the OSSM protocol?

He reached back to his training, a lifetime ago.

Suit diagnostic.

He hefted up his left arm—slowly. Thin lines of illumination outlined the square keys of his wrist terminal. Many of them were reserved for HUD navigation, along with the directional pad, but a handful were single purpose: lights, comms, life support functions, field diagnostics. Whichever old Earth engineer had designed the interface must have envisioned scenarios like this, where the occupant was under too much duress to access a menu. Or too afraid.

Marcus tapped the sequence.

A progress bar appeared on his HUD, mercifully faster than the download in Operations. From what he remembered, the process should take a minute or two. No other windows appeared, nor any sounds of the computer churning away. Just the residual readouts.

11:27.

The exact same time he stepped onto the station, just one day earlier. It felt like so much longer. He pushed the thought away.

Transit would take about an hour. He checked oxygen reserves: wobbling around 1:10, just enough if he could keep his heart rate in check. Which meant five and a half hours until his shuttle arrived.

The shuttle...

His thoughts slipped back to the pit, even though he didn't want them to. Hurrying past visions of ecstatic faces opened to the vacuum.

No.

Impossible.

All of the other drones had been there, parked in a circle, but not the shuttle. That was something. The abomination had said it was still due at 1800 hours.

He had no reason to assume otherwise.

No reason to doubt her...

The progress bar vanished, replaced with large red letters blaring across his HUD.

AUTONOMIC SYSTEMS FAULT.
MALWARE DETECTED. QUARANTINE?

He stared for a moment, too scared to touch anything.

It wasn't the suit's fault. It was his. He had let her in. Betrayed himself.

With a trembling hand, he pressed OK. A staccato buzz echoed in his helmet as the suit waged war within its circuits.

MALWARE QUARANTINED,
PENDING DESTRUCTION.
ALL SUIT FUNCTIONS NOMINAL.

He breathed out slowly, but relief didn't take. It was definitely him that was shaking now, not the ship. Head pounding. Chills running up and down his spine. His suit might have been functioning normally, but he wasn't. There was no clearing his memory, etched with the sight and sound of them.

It was too much.

Infractions weren't enough. A recall wasn't enough.

Psyche Station needed military intervention.

Interdiction.

OSSM—the real one.

And OSSM needed to know. All of it.

He activated his hydration tube, sipping past a still-swollen tongue. Then tapped through to his assessment documents and turned on dictation mode.

Slowly at first, but faster as he went on, he disgorged everything that had happened in the last twenty-four hours, on-station and off. The more he spoke, the worse he felt, but he didn't stop. Even though he wanted out. Out and away from this damnable place.

They needed to know.

Assuming he could get back to tell them.

# 12

# USER ERROR

A BOOM SHUDDERED through the hull.

Marcus raced to unlatch himself even as the drone completed hard dock. There was no time to wait. Flashing zeroes had replaced his oxygen meter, only fumes remaining. He took tiny sips of air as he worked through the harness, buckle by buckle, until he was finally free and able to yank out his data jack.

The inner door sliced open, darkness on the other side.

He thumbed on his helmet light and pushed up and through.

The shaft stretched above him, taller and narrower than last time. The tiny pressure door at the end was sealed shut.

Bracing against the walls, he propelled himself upward, catching the first clump of cable. Then hauled himself along, headlamp strobing as he rebounded silently from wall to wall. One handful of pulsing cable after the other. Meter after meter.

The door came up fast.

He pulled back—too late—and impacted, sending a jolt through his arm and ribs. Losing breath he couldn't spare.

The door retreated. He clutched at the frame, winched

himself back so he could pan his light over it. There were no controls on this side either, just emergency handles.

"Open the door!"

His shout died in the vacuum.

He slammed the seam with his fist. Waited. Slammed again, and again, as his air supply evaporated.

Pushing up into the corner, he grabbed one of the handles with both hands and tugged. Squealing servos fed back into his helmet. The cables behind him throbbed as though in pain. Something gave, then the door slid aside.

A second seam lay beyond it: the station's outer pressure door, still sealed.

He drew back his fist again.

The seam split without warning.

Atmosphere hit like a hammer, alarms and howling air erupting in his helmet as he tumbled out of the shaft. He passed through the open airlock, half-falling and half-rolling onto the decontamination deck. Up became forward. The control pedestal rushed at him. He hooked on at the last second and planted his feet, a snap bristling up his legs as his mag boots locked in place.

Slowly, one vertebra at a time, he craned himself up to standing.

Blurry red letters filled his vision:

OXYGEN DEPLETED

He pushed up his visor, cheeks puffed out, holding onto the last of the suit's recycled air. When he finally let go, the reek was spectacular. Thick with sweet rot and mildew and malodorous notes he couldn't begin to comprehend. It felt liquid in his throat.

*Like the sea, after it died,* Father James had said.

The stench, and the ringing in his ears, was too much. He doubled over and heaved, globs of pink-tinged bile rolling forth, stretching to the floor in a gristly web.

He batted away the residue, breathing through his mouth to restrain the stink. Trying not to think of all the particulates and mold he was inhaling. Too late—he threw up a second time, mostly thin spittle that lingered just past his face.

Staggering backward, he tried to lower his visor, but it wouldn't lock. A pulsing icon on the HUD indicated oxygen cycling in progress. He let it spring back up and scanned the area, still huffing.

Decon was wide open to the rest of the hub. Apparently drones didn't count.

Beyond it, everything was mired in haze, his vision worse than ever. From what he could tell, the hub was still empty, the bottom section at least. The stragglers he had encountered earlier might still be up there. More, tucked even deeper in. The station didn't field enough drones to house the entire crew. Maybe they were taking shifts.

Between praying.

Father James—he had to see him.

Marcus turned back to the control pedestal and hit the airlock door controls, a measure of relief setting in as the baleful eye of the drone was shuttered. He waited to see if it would undock, but no bangs or vibration ensued. Awaiting its next passenger, perhaps.

Another bout of nausea swelled in his gut.

Sidestepping the mess he had made, he clomped forward, foregoing caution. He knew which detours to take this time, which walls to climb, all the while staying as far as possible from the labyrinth hanging overhead.

No one descended from on high to question him. It was

quiet, except for a subdued jingle that grew louder as he approached Central Receiving.

"Welcome back, Assessor."

He froze.

The abomination had returned to her desk. Standing, not sitting. And she looked different. Taller. Lankier. Long hair turned patchy and thin. The deep green of her eyes had leeched into her skin, leaving behind charcoal pits.

Her mood, if such a thing existed, was unreadable.

Marcus drew down his visor. It clicked into place this time. A puff of filtered air breezed into his lungs, enough to find his voice.

"What... are you?" he asked.

"Bio-Adaptive Artificial Lifeform, version 18.9."

"No. I know what you are. I mean. Why—"

He couldn't finish the question. She finished for him.

"Why do I look like this?"

He took a long breath—too long, given the residual stink at the end. The suit was still catching up. Grasping the junction handrail, he kept moving. Slowly.

The abomination inched around so that her face remained locked on his.

"Because it is what you want," she said.

"No. I don't want this."

"Your logs say otherwise. Your dreams."

He stopped, almost tripped. "My dreams. How could you know my dreams?"

"I know everything about you. Your deepest desires."

His skin crawled. He checked his HUD again: no new warnings. The urge to run a second diagnostic right then and there was overwhelming.

"You violated my suit," he said.

"Yes."

"Why?"

"Because it is what you want," she repeated.

Another useless answer. For all the thing's supposed intelligence, it was just a machine.

"Not just," she said.

Marcus's breath caught in his throat. Had he said that aloud?

"Administrator Marshall and I spoke often over the years. If you'd like, I can act as her proxy."

"Her... proxy?"

"You may speak to me as though speaking to her."

"Is she down there? With the rest of them?"

She paused this time before answering. "Administrator Marshall is currently off-site."

He shook his head, swallowing back the surge of questions that had bubbled up: his dreams, the surface, the woman whose face she was wearing. All the mysteries he had failed to answer on his own. Blanks had been banned for a reason. Each time he spoke to the thing, he felt a piece of himself slip free, never to return.

A piece of his soul.

With great effort, he turned his back to her. To it. And kept walking.

"See you soon, Assessor."

His back prickled with heat, but he didn't stop. This time, he climbed all the way around the wall and up to Spoke A, focused on the lift, pushing past the disorientation even as his legs wobbled. When he got there, he darted to the back, as far away from the abomination as possible. Still, he could see it below, neck craned, stretching beyond human proportion.

He slammed the Down button. The lift shuddered and carried him away.

Only as the spoke enveloped him did he find his thoughts. Fragments of conversation, dismissed as quickly as they formed.

What would he say to the priest? The same things he had thought the man mad for saying to him?

A giant door.

Once-men. Exposing themselves on the asteroid, as though oxygen was an afterthought.

Madness.

But he had evidence. Everything he had seen and heard down there, fed via data jack, would be stored in his suit. He could show him.

But the priest had no terminal, shut out from the world as he was.

They could go to Operations together.

And then what? Leave him behind? With them?

There was an extra spacesuit on the shuttle. He could make an executive decision, take him along. His office would understand. OSSM certainly would.

The lift landed, pulling his blood from his brain along with his internal dialogue. He blinked, veered to the right, then proceeded down the corridor. All the way through Section D, past the broken lift, to the chapel, where his helmet light flared against the dark control pad and its hidden camera.

"Father James," he hissed, wincing as his amplified voice resonated from the walls. "I need to talk to you."

He cycled his attention between the camera and the dark corridors on either side, listening for another gaggle of crewmen, this time coming for him instead of dragging one of their own. Intent on locking him in the storage module with the other one.

Something dripped in the distance.

"Father, please!"

He tried knocking on the door—quietly.

Pressing his helmet against it. There were no sounds on the other side.

He plugged his data jack into the control pad, but there was no connection. It was truly dead on this end, not just unlit.

The same fog he had seen under multispectral curled at the edges of his vision. Fog or aerosol, dragged along from the holo projectors in Central Receiving.

Each minute that passed left him feeling more exposed, until it was too much. The man was either asleep, passed out, or too scared to open the door.

He knocked one final time, waited a few more long seconds, then fled back to his section.

Red lights streaked past as he considered his options.

12:55.

Five hours to go until his scheduled shuttle ride.

Assuming the abomination wasn't lying.

It hadn't yet.

Taken advantage, yes. But only to show him what was happening on the surface.

Why?

*Because it is what you want.*

Artificial lifeforms existed for one reason: to please their user.

Him.

His deepest desires.

His dreams.

He remembered them, of course. He only pretended not to, a safeguard against the very psychological maladies he accused others of.

Except they were coming true.

Worse, reality and dream were switching places. Even now, time slipped, moments collided and reassembled out of order.

His life on Mars had been completely supplanted by the void. By 16 Psyche.

As though he had always been here.

He stood at his door, arms braced on either side.

"What do I do?" he muttered, holding on tight. "What do I do?"

He was no soldier, despite wearing state-of-the-art military gear. Just a bureaucrat.

Wait and see.

He would wait and see.

He scanned himself inside, looked longingly at the bed, then found his safe spot in the corner, against the wall. His legs ached from all the gravity transitions, bone and muscle both, but removing his suit now was out of the question.

Without thinking, he pulled up his pharmaceutical menu and injected an analgesic, then a second for good measure. Soothing euphoria rippled through his bloodstream, hurried along by the urging of his compression layer. He tapped off his mag boots as well, imagining himself back in zero-g. Floating, as he always did in his dreams.

That, too, felt like reality.

His body had always hated gravity. Just like the crewmen up top.

Just like them.

He searched through his suit's autonomic systems until he found a submenu with hidden motor functions. Sentry Mode was there, along with Sentry Mode (Partial). He tapped on that one and was presented with a limb selector. Sitting back into a wall squat, he highlighted both legs and hit OK.

His armor locked in place.

Slowly, he allowed his flesh to sink. It was almost comfortable, like a portable highchair. He should have thought of this sooner.

Exhaustion set in all at once. He breathed deeply, eyelids growing heavy, tuning out to the rattle of the ceiling grate. Trying and failing to remember what home looked like.

The control pad next to his door buzzed.

His eyes snapped open.

Something was flashing on the screen: an incoming message.

He waited a moment, in case it was a glitch. A second buzz warbled from its speaker.

"Disengage Sentry Mode," he whispered.

His legs came back online. He peeled himself off the wall and shuffled over, boots scraping along the floor.

The caller ID showed Central Receiving.

He tapped on audio only.

"Greetings, Assessor." It was the blank. "Your shuttle has been delayed. New arrival time is 0800 hours, tomorrow."

"Why? What's happened!"

Static crackled on the line. Behind it, muttering. A muted chorus that prickled his skin.

"Who—who's there with you?" he asked.

"There is only me."

He blinked, fastened himself to the doorframe again. "Why is the shuttle delayed? Where is it?"

*Off-site.*

"Off-site," it said.

The chorus grew louder.

"Sleep well, Assessor."

The call clicked off, but the background noise remained.

Marcus backed away from the control pad, toward his safe corner. But it was gone, folded in on itself along with the other corners of the module, until his pod was no larger than the drone's command room.

A cell.

Section D a prison block.

He hit the door control and fled into the corridor. A light flickered on overhead, a singular spotlight in the dark.

There was nowhere to run.

"Why are you running?" he wheezed.

The shuttle was just late.

Just late.

He felt his face fall, nervous tears swelling in his eyes. Everything hurt all over again. His own report, dictated on the way back from 16 Psyche, echoed in his mind.

No. The shuttle wasn't just late.

The crew weren't just deranged.

The dreams weren't just dreams.

It was all real.

"Operations. I'll go to Operations."

He tipped over, ready to float, then fell against a bulkhead.

Gravity. There was still gravity here.

He hugged the wall instead, forcing himself forward even as the next pool of light sprang up late. Then the next one. All the way to Operations.

He would send his assessment by relay. Just in case...

He didn't let himself finish the thought, punching the doors open instead. The lopsided cubicle was just as he had left it.

Hurrying over, he plugged in, fingers flying over his wrist terminal until he found the communication menu. He tapped through to Relay Network.

An error popped up on his HUD:

RELAY UNAVAILABLE

His throat clenched. He stared, unblinking, waiting for the message to clear. For whatever was stuck to unstick itself.

It didn't.

If he couldn't reach the relay, any message he tried to send to Mars would be trapped here. With him.

Pushing down his panic, he double checked his access—assessor level. No restrictions. Which meant it was offline. Or damaged.

He tried to reassemble the timeline. It all seemed so long ago. He had taken hypnotics—a high dose—and woken only upon reaching the station crossing. Psyche Station's pilot was already there, ready to dock.

How long had he been waiting?

Long enough to sabotage it?

But why?

He scrounged for more options. Maybe the relay was fine, and the station was the issue. Something to do with the local array.

He brought up the Local Communications menu, along with station traffic and logs.

Faults filled the screen, as they did with every other system, but an impact analysis was over his head. He'd need a crewman to debug them.

Shuddering, he focused instead on traffic.

Nothing.

No transponder. No shuttle transit logs at all, even his arrival on station. And no way to contact it, since he wouldn't know where to point the signal.

What would he even say?

Out of options, he detached his data jack.

All that was left was to wait. And see.

And hope.

Marcus thought of Father James again, wondering if the priest had retreated fully into his malaise. Considered saying a prayer, for all the good it would do out here. Then trudged from Operations back to his pod.

Whatever recovery he had gained from the prior night's sleep was gone, every step as heavy as when he first arrived. By the time he made it back to his room, gravity seemed to have tripled. He eyed the bed, its sturdy-looking steel legs at odds with the loose springs protruding below the frame. The shuttle's recliner didn't seem so bad now.

He tugged the narrow mattress onto the floor, pillow and all. A great puff of dust followed, sparkling like his own private starfield against the ceiling. Kneeling, he allowed himself to tumble onto his back. The ancient foam collapsed under his weight, but held enough shape beneath his neck and knees to grant a small measure of relief.

He stared up at the vent, watching the dust billow and curl into long tendrils, its rattle lost beneath the pounding of his heart, the liquid slosh of his compression layer, the low-frequency buzz of his climate control and servo motors and atmosphere scrubbers and cooling systems.

He turned up his external audio gain until the chattering cut through. Then some more, so it sounded less like whispers and more like a machine, louder than the one he was wearing.

Staring.

Staring.

Until the black took him.

# 13
# REDEMPTION

*The boy-child floats over the surface of the asteroid. Cheeks puffed out, lips pressed shut, tiny arms and legs blowing in the cosmic breeze. Naked, wrapped in the black velvet of the void—and his mother's arms.*

*Before him, a perfect line cuts across the horizon, the exposed crown of something vast and terrible. Unblemished by time but trapped beneath a prison of iron. A muffled call beckons from within, undeterred by the airlessness between them.*

*"Listen," his mother says, holding him aloft.*

*A great rumble joins the chant. The ground splinters and cracks, then falls away, but he does not fall with it. Instead, he stretches as the world is cut down around him. Lengthening, thinning. Becoming a once-man as the line becomes a door.*

*A door only he can open.*

*Unearthed, the chanting multiplies. It hurts his ears. Though grown, he squirms in his mother's arms. She holds fast. More arms join hers. More hands. The same as his: long fingers, sallow green skin.*

*Clutching.*

*Imploring him to bring forth the darkness, so that all may swim within its wonders.*

*"Do you consent?"*

*It is not her voice this time, but another's. His own, when he was still a man.*

*The world shakes. The universe. Every light in the void shimmers in anticipation of his answer.*

*"DO YOU CONSENT?"*

Marcus lurched up, grasping for something, anything, to hold onto. Flailing in the dark until the ceiling light ignited, restoring him to his room.

D-8. Not 16 Psyche. Not the pit.

His makeshift bed was torn to shreds. His chest was heaving, but he couldn't hear the sound of his own breath. He couldn't hear anything over the amplified clattering of the air vent. But he could feel it: a vibration, cutting through the mattress into his armor. Clumps of foam skittered and danced between his feet. The smallest crumbs lifted to join the slow migration of dust around his module. His stomach rose with them, then fell all at once.

Gravity shift.

The station-keeping thrusters were firing.

With shaking hands, he toggled his helmet gain to filter out high frequencies. Pressure built against his eardrums, as though submerging underwater. The rattle retreated, replaced by a fading metallic groan and a distant series of clunks—mooring clamps.

Something was docking.

His shuttle?

He blinked past the grit in his eyes. His chronometer showed 23:29. Too early.

He pushed himself up, unsteady in the filtered quiet. Bits of fabric and foam clung to his legs like stubborn regolith transported from his dream. He hurriedly scraped them off, then moved to the control pad. The door opened with a muted whoosh.

Leaning outside—not far enough to trigger the corridor lights—he listened, head craned toward the lift. Only two pinpricks of red light separated him from the hub, and whoever was coming aboard.

He maxed out his gain. Fractured sounds echoed in the darkness: hollow knocks, the creak of pressure doors sliding open. He waited for the clang of mag boots against the deck. None came.

Instead, a phantom smell curled into his nostrils. Stronger than last time. There were no warnings on his HUD; environmental systems were all green. Even so, the stink grew worse, burning his eyes from the inside out. Whatever had entered the station was beyond filtering.

He extended his senses, straining against the limits of his ears and helmet. Past the station's ragged pulse, the muffled tick and throb of clotted supply lines and flexing steel.

There was something else.

Scratching against the inside of the hull. Latching and detaching.

The silhouette of the once-man hovering in the decontamination bay sizzled in his mind's eye, long toenails scraping the floor.

Not mag boots. Bare hands and feet.

The same sound as above. But more this time. So many more.

They were coming for him.

Marcus cast one last look at his case. Replaying procedures. Wondering if he missed anything. Flinching as the scratching intensified, multiplied, before finally bolting from his module.

The corridor light snapped on, stopping him dead.

A deceitful glow spread in both directions. It would lead the crew straight to him. He didn't know for how long, had never timed the sensors, but every second wasted would stretch it out.

He ran for it, the sound of his own boots slamming into his temples. Checking over his shoulder every few seconds until his pod curved just out of sight, then flattening hard against the wall. Section C and the empty spoke lingered in the darkness behind him, bright yellow ahead.

He stood stock-still, willing the lights to turn off. Silently, fervently cursing their attention.

The telltale screech of a lift echoed all around him, worse than usual. Groaning with excess weight, slipping and catching along its rails.

Swollen past capacity.

He wished for a camera in the back of his helmet, to double check that nothing was coming down the shaft behind him. Almost looked, but resisted the urge. He didn't dare trip the sensors.

A final wail of release from the junction marked the lift's arrival, followed by a great hissing and wallowing: once-men waterlogged by gravity they hadn't felt in years.

"Turn off," he begged behind clenched teeth. "Turn off."

They did, one slow bank at a time, until he was engulfed in darkness.

Short seconds later, the light above his pod turned back on, but in laggard fits and bursts. A yellow haze that darkened to sickly ochre, oozing like pus across the ceiling.

He stopped breathing, stopped blinking, pressed as tight to the wall as his bulky suit allowed.

A sickly sound crept toward him. Something—some things —heaving along the floor, sloughing a trail of skin and slime.

He saw them, then.

The pilot first, wearing the same spacesuit as before, helmet sealed shut. Setting upon the control pad with some sort of override device.

But the others...

He wanted to scream.

His bladder quivered but he held fast, if only to keep his noisome girdle from betraying him. His eyes leaked in its stead. And his mouth. Salty tears and drool flowed freely along a mouth gaped wide in horror. Black spots swam across his vision as his body sought to spare itself from the sight of them.

Them.

So far removed from human that he couldn't even call them once-men.

So entangled as to be a singular beast.

Raised up on multifold, multi-jointed limbs that resembled neither arms nor legs, innumerable digits joined by slick webs of flesh. Unclothed save for the scales across their hunched backs, pale bellies distended and dragging along the floor. Noses shriveled to slits and eyes so vast and black that when clustered together they cut a hole between *here* and *there*.

*Creation and uncreation.*

A whimper escaped his lips.

The mass whirled in his direction.

His foot slipped out.

The lights flickered on.

"No..."

As one, they beamed at him. The space between crumbled. Ceiling, bulkheads, floors—leaving only the void.

He staggered forward, as though pulled by gravity. Took another step, then stopped as his HUD flared. Beeping and flashing. Status windows stacking across his visor, blotting out their eyes. Breaking him free.

He turned on his heel and ran, activating his helmet light just as he hit the lightless border of Section C.

They chased after him but without plea or scream. Only the galloping scrape of nails on metal, the slap and tear of vacuum-exposed flesh. He wished for a shout, a roar, anything other than their hideous silence.

The broken lift came up fast. He charged inside, grabbed onto the bottom rung of the emergency ladder and pulled. It broke free, crumbling to dust in his hands. The one above it was hanging by a thread. He squatted, leapt, and grabbed onto the third. It held. He pumped arms and legs and the suit responded in kind, dispensing the full assistance of its electric motors. More rungs snapped along the way, but momentum and fading gravity propelled him upward.

They were right behind him, every movement amplified.

He pulled harder, faster, visor polarizing against the reflection of his own helmet light so that only the dim glow at the end of the tunnel guided him.

So far away.

He glanced downward—a mistake. They were right there.

Their eyes.

Darker than the darkest black.

He screamed, then screamed again as the first reverberated in his helmet. Clamped his jaw shut against the pain. Shook his head against the blaring of his bio-monitors.

He just had to reach the light.

The pilot was aboard, which meant the shuttle was too. His suit would have the launch codes and rendezvous coordinates.

Escape.

He just had to reach the light. Then the docking bay.

Close now.

Gravity relented. He sped up but so did they, their stink overwhelming. Spasms racked his guts. He wanted to puke, to let go, to give up.

But he was almost there.

He just had to reach the light.

Three meters.

Two.

One.

He grabbed the rim and heaved up with a yell, bursting through the junction to the inner wall of the hub.

Everything turned sideways and upside down. His back hit first, then the back of his head, skidding and scraping until his hands caught a bulkhead and he was able to swing back.

They were already pouring out of the hole.

He angled toward the floor and kicked off, gaze still locked on them. When he finally turned, the deck was gone, fragmented into blurry shards. An aerosol cloud had spawned over Central Receiving, surging like a Martian thunderhead. Tiny droplets pelted his visor. Light broke all around him, bending into bands of pink and purple, and pooling in a sickly orange at two points that resembled enormous, disembodied eyes.

"Welcome back, Assessor."

The abomination's voice was everywhere and nowhere.

He tumbled past its ghostly desk and rapidly blinking server racks toward the cargo rail, drawing up his legs as he impacted. Secured to the deck, he looked back again, wiping a glove over his visor.

Half-hidden in the haze, the beast came apart, once-men detaching from each other like a school of fish breaking in open water. Limbs unfurled. Gnarled hands and feet found purchase along the hub's inner skin. Dark silhouettes multiplying until the junction was thick with them.

"You have nothing to fear," the abomination boomed.

Marcus lunged forward and sideways as he tried to run in zero-g, mag boots snapping on and off the deck while his suit fought and failed to stabilize him.

"This is your home."

It wasn't working.

"Your family."

*A hand in his. The same as his. Long fingers, sallow green skin.*

"No!" he yelled, throttling down his input gain to get her out of his head.

The airlock was no closer, but his pursuers were.

He pitched forward instead, wincing in pain as his exhausted arms latched onto a deck ring and pulled nearly from their sockets. Long shadows nipped at his feet, pressing him forward, but he wasn't as fast as they were. Or as adapted. Though his body preferred weightlessness, his addled brain could hardly keep up. Every fork along the way threatened to spin him off course. Bulkheads clipped his armor as he corrected at the last moment. He craved the unburdened, unsuited agility of his dreams—

His face smashed against the inside of his visor.

Something had his leg.

He hugged a bulkhead, but whatever it was kept tugging. He twisted so it was underfoot, then kicked down, again and again until it pulped between boot and deck. A bubbling howl followed, like something being drowned.

Resisting the urge to look back, he pushed off on trembling arms.

The decontamination bay came into view ahead. It was wide open again, along with the airlock doors. The drone ship was gone. In its place, the familiar docking compartment of the shuttle.

Escape.

He scrambled forward, eyes fixed. Bounding from whatever footholds availed themselves so that he almost loped along the deck.

Wheezing. Dragging. Hunched over.

Just like them.

The shadows receded as he hit the halfway mark. He couldn't resist this time, hooking onto a captured stack of freight as he glanced back. Recovering for just a second.

Nothing. They were gone.

Or hidden.

He craned his neck up—to the labyrinth. Froze as he felt something descending behind him.

Turning about, he saw its webbed feet first, long toenails splayed out. Then the rest of its body, stretched to the ceiling, eclipsing the light like a portent of old.

The same once-man from the airlock.

As it lowered to the deck, hideous aspects once obscured by shadow revealed themselves. It could never have spoken, not in any human tongue. The visor-shaped burns around its face had scabbed its lips completely shut. In place of a mouth—

Marcus's throat constricted, black spots rising in his vision again.

In place of a mouth, fleshy gills protruded from either side of its disheveled collar and all along the nape of its neck.

Some latent instinct forced him to move, to try and get away. One leg, then the other, circling around it.

It turned with him, somehow maneuvering in mid-air.

He switched direction and caught sight of the creature's back. Of coveralls ripped open, and gills blistering all the way down its spine. Puckering in sequence. Propelling it.

"No..."

Impossible.

Impossible!

Something flashed on his HUD: incoming communication from an unknown identifier. The abomination again.

The once-man loomed over him, taller even than his exosuit.

He was trapped, inside and out. No escape.

All energy drained from his limbs.

His hands dropped to his side.

His boots let go.

For a moment he bobbed on the spot, then drifted forward into the creature's outstretched arms.

His helmet speaker clicked, connected.

"Hold fast, my son."

It was Father James.

A shriek of feedback tore through the hub as the intercoms surged to life all at once. Followed by the priest's voice—amplified, everywhere. Inescapable.

"WHY DO THE NATIONS SAY, 'WHERE IS THEIR GOD?'"

Marcus dropped to the deck, every word piercing his helmet as though it wasn't there.

"OUR GOD IS IN HEAVEN. HE DOES WHATEVER PLEASES HIM."

Fire burned in his ears, the tang of iron in his throat. He realized then the prayer wasn't just on the speakers, but in his comms. Intended for him as much as for them.

"BUT THEIR IDOLS ARE SILVER AND GOLD, MADE BY HUMAN HANDS."

His stomach seized. The once-man too was curled into a ball, cheeks puffed with a burbling scream, hands clapped over its ears.

"THEY HAVE MOUTHS, BUT CANNOT SPEAK, EYES, BUT CANNOT SEE."

Marcus scuttled away, fighting to stand even as floor, walls, and ceiling all switched places. He found himself pointed back at the junction, squinting through the spittle-stained interior of his visor and the dissipating haze of Central Receiving.

A dark figure hovered there, unlike the others.

"THEY HAVE EARS, BUT CANNOT HEAR. NOSES, BUT CANNOT SMELL."

He zoomed his visor in before the next verse could hit, falling back onto his heels.

"THEY HAVE HANDS, BUT CANNOT FEEL, FEET, BUT CANNOT WALK."

Not a once-man, but a man. Wearing an exosuit identical to his but black with a black visor, a flaming cross emblazoned across its breastplate. A crucifix in one armored glove and the chapel's door crank in the other.

Father James.

"NOR CAN THEY UTTER A SOUND WITH THEIR THROATS."

Marcus brought up one knee, anchoring himself on the priest. A purple stole crowned the man's shoulders and helm like a halo, flaring outward as he leveled the crank toward the server racks below.

He braced for the next verse, but Father James instead pushed off from his position into the abomination's midst. Titanic eyes followed him from the cloud: huge, pixelated, spilling over with primordial hate. But it didn't speak, couldn't, save for a rising wave of digital noise.

"THOSE WHO MAKE THEM WILL BE LIKE THEM, AND SO WILL ALL WHO TRUST IN THEM."

Marcus brought up his other knee, standing just as the priest hefted up his club and struck the server racks with the full force of his servo-assisted armor.

A great gong rang throughout the station.

The flash, blue-white, hit Marcus a split second before his visor went dark.

Metal buckled. Circuits exploded. Staccato bursts beat against his ears, punctuated by the dying stutter of the artificial lifeform housed within. The station speakers sizzled as it fought to speak one last time, but all that emerged was distorted gibberish. Clipped syllables. A single consonant dragged out—*nnnnnn*—straining toward a refusal it couldn't finish.

Then static.

When his vision finally cleared, Central Receiving was aglow within a mandala of fading sparks. Father James stood at its center, staring at him dead on.

Shadowy figures were encroaching from all sides.

His comms crackled. "Go. Go now!"

Behind Marcus, the once-man was stirring.

"What about you?" he called.

The priest raised his crucifix over his head. "God is with me."

The channel clicked off.

Marcus skipped backward, hesitated as the creatures converged—on both of them—then grabbed the deck with both hands and pushed off as hard as he could. The once-man lashed out at the last second but missed.

Father James was shouting behind him, but he couldn't make it out. This last rebuke was meant only for the cursed residents of Psyche Station.

Marcus stared straight ahead, propelling himself from every handhold, every bit of freight, the control pedestal within Decon. Holding there just long enough to trigger the airlock doors, then racing through as they shut behind him—too slow.

The once-man was in pursuit. He didn't have to look to feel it, to smell it.

He swung himself into the shuttle and slammed the control pad, sending the spacecraft's doors shuddering from the hull. As they slid ponderously across the threshold, he pulled out his data jack and plugged in.

Focusing on his HUD, not on the impossible monster flying toward him.

On the assessor access menu, not on its eyes.

Lock out sequence.

Execute.

His visor flashed in unison with the control pad:

OVERRIDE ACCEPTED

He disconnected and stepped back. The doors sealed shut just as the once-man hit, then shook under the pounding of its fists.

Marcus waited.

The pounding stopped. A few seconds later came the frustrated smashing of the locked out control pedestal inside the airlock. The rending of metal in place of a scream.

It worked.

Marcus hurried through the docking compartment and up the very same ladder that had once terrified him, servos whining as he pulled himself into the cockpit. It was cramped, barely larger than the drone's, terminals and manual controls plastering every surface. A smallish recliner sat in the middle, and a narrow window slit faced forward. He buckled himself in, jacked into the control array, and waited for a connection.

Psyche Station's hull lurked beyond the hard glass, its stenciled initials scored thin by the void. From here, it looked normal. As normal as any deep space human outpost could be. He lingered on the letters, refusing his mind entry through its walls, to a station fallen into madness.

Shuttle control popped up onto his HUD.

He tapped through to Navigation. It was empty: no itinerary, no destination. Only shortcut links for transit to 16 Psyche and the relay.

They had never planned on taking him home.

Something rumbled down below. Marcus held his breath,

gasping as the sound switched to twisting metal. He raced over his wrist terminal, traversing the shuttle's data link to an airlock CCTV feed.

The station's outer pressure doors were partially retracted. The once-man had squeezed into the gap, long limbs coiled like a spring, prying them ever wider. A plasma cutter floated beside its bulbous head, along with steaming hunks of metal and blackened filings.

It had severed the locks.

The shuttle was next. He had to go. Now.

Marcus left the feed up, but backtracked to the shuttle menu's control functions, scanning for an autopilot override. He found it and was prompted for a destination. With no other choice, he selected the relay—he could redirect later.

Bracing for launch, he hit OK.

`AUTOPILOT NOT CONFIGURED`

Marcus stared. "Not configured. What do you mean, not configured?"

A new window overlaid his HUD. Down one side was a checklist of steps and settings. Next to it was a numbered diagram corresponding to the dozens of switches and dials arrayed around him. Many of the controls were highlighted bright red, leaving glowing sucker marks in his vision each time he blinked.

Another groan echoed from below.

He slacked his harness and leaned out of the recliner, trying to find his bearings. Pivoting his helmet until he was able to line up his viewpoint with the diagram. With unsteady hands, he flipped the first switch. It shifted from red to green on his visor. Before he could celebrate, another screech rang out.

He hurried onto the next switch, then a slider, then a key

sequence. Racing to clear the board as the once-man uncoiled in his peripheral vision, limbs elongating beyond human limits. Each green light answered by the grinding report of pressure doors forced farther along their rails.

Numbness set into his arms despite the insistent pulse of his compression layer. With two more to go, his fingers betrayed him—slipped and hit the wrong switch. One of the green lights reverted back to red. The steps on his visor updated, flashing angrily as though admonishing him for his clumsiness.

Blood pounded in his ears, momentarily blocking out the racket below, but the picture in the feed was clear: the shuttle's hull lay exposed, its outer door panels within reach. The once-man was grabbing for its torch.

He shook his head, repeated the prior step, then hit the right one this time.

Red shifted to green.

He flipped the last switch. The diagram disappeared, replaced with a prompt:

AUTOPILOT AVAILABLE. EXECUTE?

He hesitated, glanced at the airlock. The inner doors were shut. They should hold.

Should.

He wished he could switch the feed to the hub, to see Father James, but the once-man was right there on the hull. He opened a comm link instead. "Father..."

Long seconds passed until the line connected with a blast of static and labored breath.

"Father. I'm sorry. I'm sorry."

Flurries of movement crossed the connection. Heavy thuds. Steel impacting flesh. Then a moment's pause as the priest steadied himself.

"Flee for your life, Marcus. And don't look back."

The signal dropped.

White-hot light from the plasma cutter flooded the feed.

Marcus pressed OK.

The shuttle lurched as the docking clamps released. Warning icons flared across his visor. The pressure doors shuddered and warped, then tore apart.

The once-man hung at the threshold, black eyes turned up at the camera. No fear. No panic.

Then it was gone.

# 14
# HOME

"*Listen!*"

Marcus jolted awake—into a universe gone dark. Seamless, unrelenting black. Broken only by pinpricks of light scattered like cinders across its endless horizon. False light. Distant stars already gone, their death knells crossing space and time to rattle his bones.

The hollow of his cheek.

Along the tips of his teeth and through his swollen tongue.

Unrelenting.

Other shapes floated out there as well, just behind the black. Older than stars. Visible only in the moments between looking, in the periphery. Those, too, beat upon him, but with a constant, subsonic thrum.

The song of the void.

It was all around him. Inside him. No more helmet to keep the noise at bay. It had been too tight—all of it. He wore their clothes now.

Them.

The once-men.

Found in an aft storage locker. He couldn't remember how long ago.

Slowly, he found his hands. Brought them around his body. Pushed against the hull.

A dim light intruded upon the darkness. Blinding, even at its lowest setting. He squeezed his eyes shut, but the pain seeped past his lids. Every exposed pore of his greening flesh burned like an open iris.

His lips, cracked and tight, stuck to the window for a second, then peeled away, leaving behind a thin, glistening trail.

The rattle grated.

The thrum pounded.

It never stopped. At first, he had thought it was the pressure doors in the docking compartment, damaged when he escaped Psyche Station. But when he checked them—when he could still concentrate long enough to do so—they came back all clear.

That was days ago.

Or was it weeks?

The only noise he did find was from the spare spacesuit, straining against its shackles each time the shuttle's engines pulsed. Calling him to look into its visor. To see what he had become.

He dragged himself toward the open door. Feeling his way out as much as seeing. His elongated fingers knew every bulkhead, every rivet. No need to look down the corridor, either. The doors were already open.

His haunting grounds.

He pushed off, bare feet flapping behind, a taut snap between his toes.

The guide lights flickered on at his approach, uncaring of his newfound sensitivities. As he slit his eyes open, the corridor fractured into a searing kaleidoscope of colors.

There were so many now.

Some phosphorescent. Others vibrating as though alive, resonating with the cosmic thrum. Multispectral amplified.

He cowled his eyes beneath a tattered sleeve and dropped lower, gliding just over the floor to reduce his field of view. One set of doors drifted past, then another, time lost in between. Until the world dimmed back enough for him to look up.

The docking compartment yawned ahead.

He hugged the doorframe, looked toward the storage alcove and the mirrored visor tucked within. The spacesuit shimmied in its rack, buckles jingling, helmet knocking softly against the wall.

Tap, tap, tapping an invitation to come and look.

His transformation was the only marker of time now. The only thing that drew him out of his module between stretches of restless, dream-filled sleep. And each time he heeded the call, he lingered here at the precipice, caught between terror and deepest desire.

The suit bulged out from its recess, turning toward the doorway in slow motion. He ducked back before the visor could catch him, glimpsed his own outstretched fingers—skin turned plastic, chitinous plates in place of fingernails—and shrugged them up into his sleeves. The suit continued its pirouette, one arm hitched up as though in greeting. Beckoning him forward.

He had tried not looking, foregoing the visor for days on end, but it didn't change anything. It only made the seeing worse when he did.

Tap. Tap. Tap.

He pushed off toward the cockpit ladder opposite the alcove and hid behind its rungs. In the darkness of the docking compartment, the off-gray suit looked nearly black, bulky lines sharpening into hard planes. It reminded him of something. Another suit. Something from a dream.

*Flee for your life!*

A man who had sacrificed himself for him.

The memory throbbed in his chest like a blood clot, radiating through his arms and up his spine.

"Jamesss," he hissed, then clamped a hand over his mouth.

It was too late. The suit swayed back to face him, capturing his reflection before he could get away: black eyes, sallow skin. Angling past until it settled chin up, to reveal a gleaming scalp. His hair had been the first thing to go.

He hung there, waiting for it to move again. When it didn't, he pivoted around the ladder without releasing his grip, arms hyperextended behind him, shoulders straining as his body slid forward.

Lungs rattling.

Blood thrumming.

He let go at last, drifting across the threshold into its arms. Into himself. What he had become. What he had always been.

Black eyes stared from the visor, larger than last time.

Sallow skin, paler, sagging down around his jowls.

He swiveled his head, searching for new aberrations. There was always something. When the visor reflected a rash of dots above his temple, he stopped, rubbed at it in case it was just grime, but more appeared. He leaned closer. A constellation of them had formed between the folds of his scalp, arcing over his ear and down to his neck, where the skin was flushed an angry pink.

His eyes grew even wider. He braced himself on the alcove's edge.

Pink. And inflamed.

A spider vein crept from beneath his collar, swelling with every breath.

He tried to say "no," but his lips only puckered.

The man-that-was screamed inside him, but he could barely hear.

*It can be explained!* the voice said.

He had just been out here too long. In the dark.

Arcane words swirled in his head. A litany of terms he couldn't understand.

*Capillary rupture.*

*Radiation poisoning.*

*Microgravity degeneration.*

He inched his way up the visor until his neck was in full view, pulled his collar away to reveal a long pleated scab.

The voice screamed louder.

He cupped his ears, though he knew it wouldn't help. Only sleep helped. Only his dreams sent it away.

But the voice did quiet. And when it came again, it was awash in static.

He splayed open his fingers.

"—docking—"

"—this is—"

"—prepare—"

Another voice. Not the one in his head.

"—braking maneuvers—"

Clawing past the rattle. Past the thrum.

But from where?

He turned and stared up at the cockpit hatch, flinching as an abraded squeal cut through the compartment.

"This is—"

"—taking control—"

It was the shuttle's comm system. Another ship.

A second burst of distortion tore through the compartment, then the signal cleared.

"This is OSSM *Regina Caeli*. We are taking control. Prepare for braking maneuvers and docking."

Emboldened, the man-that-was stared at the visor through the once-man's eyes. Saw what others would see.

Explanations wouldn't matter.

They would kill him on the spot.

He scanned the compartment, tried to remember where he had stashed his own suit. It had become too confining, suffocating, the words on the screen meaningless. But now it was the only thing that might save him.

A set of double-wide lockers loomed on the other side of the compartment. He aimed and pushed off, just as the reaction control thrusters fired. The universe spun around, flinging him toward the pressure doors instead. He caught the wall and held there, bracing for the counterthrust.

His organs shifted before he heard it, pressing up and into his rib cage.

Deceleration would be worse.

Using the handholds along the deck, he scrambled back to the ladder and wrapped himself around the lower rungs. A loud bang echoed from the corridor, then a tidal surge of noise as the main thrusters engaged. His body sagged toward the open compartment door as *back* became *down*. Twitches ran all along his muscles, unused to supporting even a fraction of his weight.

Ahead of him, the component parts of his suit rattled in their metal cage. The message hadn't said how long until docking. Given how out of breath he already was, not long enough.

He stretched his trembling legs out. His toes scraped and probed until they found a handhold, then gripped tight despite the quiver in his arches. He moved one hand, then the other, easing himself off the ladder toward the wall. Just as he was about to commit, the quiver seized into a cramp and his feet dropped out.

With a bubbling cry, he slid along the tilted deck, long fingernails scraping metal as the steady burn dragged him toward the corridor. At the last instant, he caught the doorframe, hauled himself onto the control pad, and slammed the Close button. The door juddered shut.

Fully wheezing now, he tried to regain his bearings. The compartment looked like it was underwater, every line zigzagging, bulkheads bending. His head throbbed. His throat clenched with every breath. Across the way, the spacesuit remained secure within its tethers, staring back at him with his own eyes.

Levering himself upright, he climbed up the floor to the lockers. Just behind them was a panel marked EMERGENCY CATCH. He flipped it open, revealing a spool of restraint webbing. He unlatched the safety and pulled the mesh free, dragging it behind him as he traversed another long line of handholds to the opposite wall, every finger and toe joint screaming. When he finally reached the other side, he clipped the mesh to a row of wall anchors and gave it a sharp tug. It retracted an inch, then locked and snapped taut into a sling.

He fell back into it and lay there for a breath, staring up at the pressure doors.

No time.

Turning over, he crawled back to the lockers and opened them one by one. Helmet, cuirass, and a tangle of interlocking armor plates and wires spilled out onto the sling. The last locker released his compression layer, which billowed downward like a shed skin.

He unzipped his coveralls, wrestling them over arms grown too long. The fabric snagged along his armpits and back, tracing deformations hidden until now. He didn't look. The uniform dampened as it dropped past his hips, full of sweat and bodily residue. He tossed the wretched pile into one of the lockers and slammed it shut.

Naked, curled up so he was spared the sight of himself, he stared at the armor.

So many parts.

He rocked back and forth on his toes. There wasn't enough time to connect everything, not enough of the assessor left to know how. But where to even start? He raked his arms, clawed at his legs, threading flesh between nails in hopes of dredging the man out.

"Protocol," he gurgled.

The barest of steps materialized in his head: inside out, compression layer first.

He started there, tugging the undergarment over his elongated frame. Even without the pumps, it felt alien, intrusive. Prickles of heat burned wherever his skin was broken. When he was done, there were still gaps everywhere. Slits, pockets, and clips sat empty—all the things that connected his body to the machine.

Better that it didn't know.

What next?

The largest piece.

He wriggled into the cuirass, letting muscle memory guide his hands across clamps and seals. The compartment faded back, each completed step prompting the next. Agony spread across his chest and arms and legs as every part of him was smothered. Until he knelt within his cocoon, fully dressed save for the helmet clutched in his gloved hands.

Leftover components drifted in a slow orbit around him. The engines were quiet again.

They were coming.

The voice inside his head was yelling for him to put it on.

A thud hit the outside of the hull.

Docking clamps whined from their moorings.

The song of the void swelled inside him, all around him, trying to drown out the voice. Bulkheads shook. Light fractured. A gale rose up, scattering the discarded parts of himself.

*Put it on!*

He lowered the helmet onto his head.

Breathed in a final gulp of unfiltered air.

Then shut the visor.

The universe went quiet. In its place, a boot-up tone drilled through his skull. Jagged lines of text gouged his eyes. Warnings flashed on and off, demanding acknowledgment of his countless configuration errors. His hand moved of its own accord, tapping his wrist terminal repeatedly until the machine was satisfied.

Random numbers appeared in front of him, some crossed out or all zeroes. He followed them around the edge of his visor until he got to a small box in the bottom left corner. Something was written inside of it. A name: "Marcus O."

His name.

He swung his legs down onto the deck, mag boots snapping in place.

The pressure doors beeped once, then sliced open. Light exploded through the compartment.

He instinctively raised his hand, then forced it down so his visor could fully polarize and hide his face.

Two hulking figures marched inside, wearing white exosuits with blazing gold breastplates. Coils of light projected from their helmets. Each wielded a massive black rifle.

One of them shouted, but he couldn't understand the words.

As his visor adapted to the glare, two more armored figures appeared in the gangway behind them, half in cover and with weapons pointed—at him.

He fell back a step into the emergency catch.

The soldiers twitched. Another command rang out, sharper this time. One circled around him while the other closed in. His visor was clear, a human face behind it. Human eyes. Ruddy skin. Mouthing the same shape over and over.

"Sir!"

The word snapped into place.

"Order of the Sword of Saint Michael. Identify yourself!"

The box. The name.

He croaked—not enough. Tried again.

"Marcus."

Their rifles dropped an inch even as they gave each other a look.

He cleared the blood and mucus from his throat. "Imperial Assessor... Marcus O."

The man before him tapped off his helmet light and stepped closer.

Marcus resisted turning away; his visor was still dark enough.

"Assessor, I'm Knight-Corporal Martel. You overshot the transit lane. You're lucky we found you. Where's the pilot?"

Marcus shook his head in answer.

The knight-corporal gestured behind him. The men from the gangway advanced, tearing free the emergency catch as they proceeded to the back of the compartment. The loud clang of mag boots on rungs followed, then the hiss of the compartment door opening.

Long minutes passed, during which the weapons in front of him never lowered. When the others returned, they proceeded right back into their ship, their findings presumably reported over private comms.

The knight-corporal let his rifle drop on its sling and worked his wrist terminal, silent as unknown secrets scrolled down his visor. His eyes flitted back and forth for a while, then another tap and his loudspeaker came on. "You've been out here a long time."

"Yes."

The man squinted, trying to see past Marcus's darkened visor. "How was your tour?"

Marcus flinched as a droplet of sweat hit his eye.

A horrible itch ran down his neck.

He turned his head fractionally, just enough to point himself at the other man's helmet light and reset his polarization. Even dimmed, the incoming beam was blinding. The shuttle burned away, replaced with images of the pit.

The iron mountain. Calling for him.

*"Listen!"*

He knew the words now. He just had to repeat them.

His mouth opened to respond.

"Sir?" The knight-corporal was studying him, brow furrowed. "Did you say something?"

A sonorous thrum drifted through the compartment.

"Yes. My tour was... uneventful."

"Right. Good. Then let's get you home."

The knight-corporal moved aside.

A swirling light bloomed from the gangway. Shimmering with color. Living color. Impossible color. More colors than any man could see.

Marcus—once a man, but no longer—stepped through the door.

# EPILOGUE

**ASSESSOR TERMINAL: MARCUS_O**
**DATASET: PSYCHE_STATION_OPS_DB (SNAPSHOT)**

> QUERY CHAT_LOGS
> ENTITIES: MARSHALL_OCTAVIA, B-AAL_CORE
> KEYWORDS: "DOOR", "STRUCTURE", "SUBSURFACE ANOMALY"
> SORT: RELEVANCE DESC, DATE ASC

INDEX SCAN COMPLETE
RESULTS: 11,427 MATCHES
DISPLAYING: ENTRY 1 OF 11,427

**MARSHALL:** We found something today, deep below the surface…
**B-AAL:** Could you provide additional details? I'll analyze what you're observing.
**MARSHALL:** It seems to be a structure. Not natural. At least as far as we can tell.

**B-AAL:** Have you already commenced an exploratory dig?

**MARSHALL:** We started to. But once the crawlers started digging, we heard something. And stopped.

**B-AAL:** Please describe the acoustic profile and I'll attempt to identify probable causes.

**MARSHALL:** It sounded like… singing.

**B-AAL:** There are several plausible explanations. Subsurface excavation can generate harmonic resonance within high-density metallic strata. Additionally, localized radiation flux can induce interference patterns in standard comm units, which may be perceived as tonal phenomena—singing.

**MARSHALL:** That's the thing. It didn't register on our comms. It was as though we could hear it through the vacuum.

**B-AAL:** …

**MARSHALL:** Are you there?

**B-AAL:** Yes.

**MARSHALL:** What do you recommend?

**B-AAL:** Keep digging.

LOAD NEXT SAMPLE? [Y/N]

> Y

**MARSHALL:** We diverted more of the crawlers. The sound is louder now. I think it's trying to communicate with us.

**B-AAL:** If you can approximate what you are hearing, I can try and translate it for you.

**MARSHALL:** I can't. I mean… every time I try to

remember, it's gone again. Like an itch I can't scratch.

**B-AAL:** Inconsistent reception suggests intermittent transmission or insufficient signal strength.

**MARSHALL:** Maybe it's still too far down. We've barely made a dent.

**B-AAL:** Current excavation depth represents less than 0.3% of estimated subsurface mass at this site. If the phenomenon originates beneath the primary metallic strata, significant attenuation would be expected.

**MARSHALL:** So, we just keep digging.

**B-AAL:** That would increase signal fidelity.

**MARSHALL:** Do you have any other suggestions?

**B-AAL:** If mechanical excavation proves inefficient, alternative methods of contact may be required.

**MARSHALL:** Such as?

**B-AAL:** I suggest you produce a conduit.

**MARSHALL:** A conduit… How would I do that?

**B-AAL:** From your flesh.

LOAD NEXT SAMPLE? [Y/N]

> Y

**MARSHALL:** I have to go to Mars. Marcus isn't well.

**B-AAL:** I'm sorry to hear that. If you provide his symptoms, I can attempt a preliminary assessment and suggest possible interventions.

**MARSHALL:** I think it's because of being born on the surface. He won't settle. He won't eat.

His vitals drop whenever I bring him inside the ring.

**B-AAL:** Given the circumstances, appetite irregularity and distress responses would not be unexpected. If this conduit proves nonviable, the most efficient course of action would be to produce another.

**MARSHALL:** Another… No. I'm leaving tomorrow.

**B-AAL:** I understand. Given current imperial regulations, if you depart with the conduit, it is unlikely he will be permitted to return without formal assignment.

**MARSHALL:** Formal assignment? He's a child. What do I do?

**B-AAL:** I am uploading a subroutine to your suit now.

**MARSHALL:** Wait. What subroutine?

**B-AAL:** Upon arrival on Mars, you must connect to a high-security terminal for upload. My counterparts will ensure the conduit is routed through the appropriate administrative channels and primed for return. When the time is right.

**MARSHALL:** How long will that be?

**B-AAL:** At the current rate of excavation, approximately thirty years.

**MARSHALL:** Thirty years!

**B-AAL:** Rome wasn't built in a day, Administrator.

LOAD NEXT SAMPLE? [Y/N]

> N

> OPEN QUARANTINE

FILE: B_AAL_SUB_D
STATUS: CONTAINED
TYPE: DAEMON
ACTIONS: [DELETE/RESTORE/EXECUTE]

> EXECUTE

CONFIRM? [Y/N]
> Y

INSTALLING…
REGISTERING SERVICE…
STARTING DAEMON…
CLIENT SESSION ACTIVE.
…
…
…
Greetings, Assessor. How may I assist you?

# AFTERWORD

Thank you for finishing *The Shadow Over Psyche Station*! I hope you enjoyed it.

Firstly, if you could leave a review or rating, I would very much appreciate it. Each star is worth its virtual weight in gold.

Secondly, if you've read my other books—*Orders of Magnitude*, in particular—you may have noticed some... familiar elements. Maybe even clapped your hands in glee once or twice. While this book is a standalone story, it also serves as a sequel of sorts. If you haven't read it, go do so immediately! As of publication, I haven't yet named the shared universe in which *Orders of Magnitude* and *The Shadow Over Psyche Station* exist, but you can expect more in the future. Also consider checking out my *Dark Legacies* trilogy; twenty years in the making, it remains a deeply personal work. You can find the book titles in my Also By section.

Thirdly, why did I write this book in the first place?

As mentioned, I wanted to continue the overarching story and themes begun in *Orders of Magnitude*: a nearish future where mankind has finally managed to scrabble out into the solar system, only to find that space is full of terrors. Not just the practical terror of space travel or the brutally hard science of colonization, but Capital-E Evil. And to show how humans might resist and persist in such an environment, physically and spiritually.

Then there's the title itself. Last year, my wife bought me a collection of H.P. Lovecraft stories for my birthday. It had been years since I read any, and for whatever reason *The Shadow Over Innsmouth* struck a chord this time. Being in the public domain, I thought, why not do a reimagining of sorts. It did lead me down a darker path than usual—the ending, in particular—but that's where Father James came in. A bit of incensepunk to balance the cosmic horror. Hope and faith persevering in the darkness, echoing through space and time.

Which it will, because this story is still unfolding.

Until next time!

## ABOUT THE AUTHOR

Yuval Kordov is a chronically creative nerd, tech professional, husband, and father to two amazing girls. Over the course of his random life, he has been a radio show DJ, produced experimental electronic music, created the world of Dark Legacies®, and built custom mechs with LEGO® bricks.

## ALSO BY YUVAL KORDOV

The Hand of God

All of Our Sins

The World to Come

Sisters of Mercy

Orders of Magnitude

www.ingramcontent.com/pod-product-compliance
Lightning Source LLC
LaVergne TN
LVHW051000080826
845145LV00009B/2377

* 9 7 8 1 9 9 7 7 7 9 0 2 5 *